I STOMP ON YOUR THROAT

Dr. Bronco F. Hammer

Sierra West Books

ISBN 13: 978-1-892798-33-6

Cover design by: Hammer Design Shop
Cover models: John Rolfe and stock photos
Interior photographs: Hammer Design Shop
Weapon Consultants: Jeff Trapp and Carlo DeBlasio
Review team: Randy Lewis
Official cocktail for this publication: Manhattan
Chief Engineer: Tony Chamberlain
Senior musical advisor: Raven Douglas

Firearm errors are on me, not the advisory team. I usually just ignore their advice.

Dedicated to LAPD Sergeant Al Powell ... Hero of the terrorist attack on Nakatomi Plaza 1988...
And
To my brothers and sisters of the MPD-SIU, or SID, or whatever you dirtbags are calling yourselves now... Much love...
And
To my faithful readers, thank you for paying my dock fees and bar tabs. I will never let you down.

"The essential American soul is hard, isolate, stoic, and a killer."
D.H. Lawrence

Being a cop leaves a stain on your soul that can never be washed away
Unknown

"Say what you will about the 32ACP, but when somebody shoots you in the nuts at point blank range, the ballistics charts do not come in to play."
Dr. Bronco F. Hammer – the most dangerous writer in the world

CONTENTS

PRE-READ BRIEFING

Okay, everyone... find a chair, sit down, and listen up.

This book guides us into the bowels of Los Angeles, California where we discover a world of crime, filth, and corruption. We'll face a level of brutal and ruthless violence that normal people might find unimaginably awful. But it will be fine. Most of us old school types are used to it. At one time or another we've all had to slap down the kinds of maggots you will find in this story. But within the pages of this incredible piece of sophisticated action literature, we can allow the protagonist to handle the gnarly stuff while we sip whiskey and read.

As is the usual case with my stories, our hero is a dirt bag. As you well know, it often takes someone who is a bit of a dirt bag to deal with the worst of the worst in the real world. It isn't pretty, dearest readers... it's ugly. It's Los Angeles ugly. I think you get the point. I see you all nodding knowingly as you sip your delicious beverages.

We will also discover that our story this time is a morality tale for those who might think about messing with our country. If you have concerns about dealing with our good... wait till you meet the bad. And the ugly standing over there in the shadows sharpening his knife? You don't even want to know... trust me.

"America."

I wish to avoid any spoilers, so I'll keep this brief. Get another cocktail, a helmet, and put on a bullet-resistant vest before reading.

Wait a minute... you... over there... reading this while you're sitting on the pot... get your ass to the living room in your recliner with your faithful dog, a cigar, and a supermodel like the rest of the readers... what the hell's wrong with you?

Sorry, I had to take some corrective action with a new reader... back to the book.

This is a typical down and dirty Los Angeles So-Cal Noir Detective story, so expect a lot of pointless violence, bad language, and bad traffic. That's it. Enjoy the story. You are clear to start reading. Best of luck and thank you for being a customer.

Your pal,

Bronco Hammer – The most dangerous writer in the world

PS: This all takes place a week before Christmas, so it's a Christmas story. I won't mention it much in the book though.

PROLOGUE

My name is John Deddario. On the streets of Los Angeles, they call me Johnny Dedd.

I hurt people for money. Sometimes I kill people for money. Once in a while I kill people just because they need killing.

It's what I do, and I do it very well.

I'm not nice.

I'm for hire.

CHAPTER 1

PAIN

I woke up. Something was wrong.

My face hurt. Faces aren't supposed to hurt.

I attempted and failed to roll my sorry ass out of bed.

This is why nobody likes mornings.

Flopping over on my belly didn't help. It made it worse. I sprawled out across the mattress, fighting a nearly overwhelming urge to barf my guts out. The night before started coming back to me... a little hazy... but I remembered. Some asshole, a very large asshole, called me a loser.

I'm not a loser. I explained that fact to him very politely. Being a professional requires staying calm during a crisis. I told him I wasn't there to argue, my job was to deliver a message about his delinquent gambling debt and to invite him to take a walk to an ATM with me. I needed him to pay some of what was due as an act of good faith on his part and I would move on to the next deadbeat.

Then there was a fight. It didn't go well for me. In physics there is this thing about mass times velocity squared. He had a lot of mass and a lot of velocity. He used every bit of it to sucker punch me. I landed square on my ass with a bent beak on my face. Turns out he was a sparring partner for a professional fighter. He certainly wasn't a boxing champion himself, yet he was clearly not some-one a non-professional fighter would want to go toe to toe with.

So, it's true. I might have lost a fist fight... embarrassing, but not the first time that happened. But in my defense, I won the subsequent knife fight.

All's well that ends well. Except my client won't see more than the five hundred bucks my opponent had in his pocket.

I believe it's fair to say that I'd rather have my nose flattened than get a shiv jabbed into my guts. At least I came home alive. But a bent snout still hurts. Science tells us that the nose is one of the most sensitive organs of the body... First is the testicles and then the nose. I think I read that somewhere. It might have been on the Internet, so I believe it's true. Or was it the history channel? It doesn't matter. It's probably true. It feels true.

My face hurts. Faces aren't supposed to hurt.

Rising slowly to an upright position and listing slightly to starboard, I shakily rose to my feet. My thoughts were odd and somewhat incoherent. I tried to focus... but the sound... it was awful.

Is that a pack of pissed off cops banging on my door an-

nouncing a search warrant?

No dumbass… That's your head pounding.

Kill me now. Make it quick.

Great, now my inner-dialogue is suicidal.

I stuck the little automatic from the nightstand into the top of my boxers as I made way for the head. I don't go anywhere without a gun these days. Although these were older skivvies, they didn't have holes in them, so they stayed in the underwear rotation even though they were a size or so too small. I'd put on some weight since my long past prime days during the academy. Not much, but some. It all worked out. The weapon was safely snugged between my ever so slightly expanding gut and the tightening ancient elastic waistband with no chance of slipping out.

How tactical is that? Even though I might be facing imminent death here, I am still ready for action. That's how a bad ass rolls.

My discomfort soon overwhelmed my random moment of macho madness.

There is something about a sore face that really sucks, and I'll tell you why. You can't smear tiger balm on it. You can't wrap it with an Ace Bandage. It's one of those injuries you have to just cope with… Some of my friends who were veterans might say, embrace the suck. But I don't believe that crap about embracing suck or about pain being weakness leaving the body. Whoever thought that nonsense up apparently was never told that pain hurts.

But at least there's ibuprofen. I keep four bottles of 500 pills stocked in the bathroom cupboard at all times. They don't last long.

The journey continues. To fully conduct an examination of my tenderized kisser, I had to survive a long trip to the head.

I trudged the cruelly long and somewhat ironic twelve steps to the bathroom, completing my journey at the sink, and flipped on a light. I blinked into the glare of three 60 watt bulbs mounted above the mirror and took a hard look at myself... *Ewww... Not good...*

As I remember, my nose is supposed to be closer to the center of my face. The dirtbag from the alley behind the strip club caught me square with a sucker punch that had the force of a well swung two-by-six Douglas Fir framing stud. He flattened my snot locker with that cheap shot. Then he tried to slice and dice me like a Vegomatic salesman working over a stack of cucumbers at the county fair. I hope the rude jerk felt like that shit was worth the cost.

Asshat.

I splashed some water on my face. Some other events from my previous evening started coming back a bit more clearly now. My perspective slowly expanded beyond my nose and hangover. I didn't just get drunk and get into a fight. I totally killed that guy.

Whoopsie.

God, I hope there isn't any blowback on this crap.

Was it murder? No, not even close. It was a nice, clean, tidy case of self-defense. He pulled his blade first; I used mine faster. I was on the ground, dazed from the sucker punch when he tried to finish me with a nasty looking fixed blade knife. I flipped open my Model 294 Momentum Spring Assisted Buck knife with its stubby steel blade. Short, but effective. Sharp, and lethal. I deflected his thrust, swept his arm aside, stabbed him in the carotid artery, and pushed him off the top of me. He flopped over on his back twitching and spraying blood like a pussy, so I got up and kicked him in the nuts out of an abundance of caution.

All legal, like I said, but with my history, I don't need the police involved in my current business model.

There was better than a seventy-five percent chance that I'd never even hear about this little misunderstanding again. If no one happened to notice the carcass in the dumpster, his mortal remains would make a one-way trip from trash bin, to trash truck, and on to the land fill where he would disappear forever as unidentifiable flattened goo smooshed between an assortment of disgusting garbage and junk.

Enough reflection... My face hurts.

It was time to repair the damage to the what is perhaps the most perfect example of a masculine face ever created. My beautiful Italian mug. First a handful of ibuprofen... then I grabbed my nose tightly and braced.

One, two, three, go!

The sound of twisting cartilage almost made me puke.

One hard yank and the bent snoz was popped back in place.

Ouch!

My eyes began watering. I blinked out the involuntary leakage... totally not tears... just an involuntary response to a medical stimulus... *owwww*... I did a little impromptu dance. *Owwww..*

After the initial pain began to subside, I lit up a Lucky Strike and examined my work...

Damn, Johnny Deddario is one handsome Italian... except maybe for the nose part.

I'd need to put some ice on it. The swelling was less than flattering.

I baby-stepped sleepily to the kitchen and grabbed a bag of frozen veggies out of the freezer and slapped a frosty sack of soothing snow peas on my face. I dumped a dozen more ibuprofen in a glass, added a shot of Jack, topped off the vessel with half a bottle of pink Pepto, guzzled it, and then limped back to bed for another hour of sleep.

Why did I limp when my nose was hurt, you ask? Because it makes me feel better. Shut up, asshole. This is like a man-flu situation. Critical incident level shit.

Sixty-eight minutes later I was up again, a new man.

Next tasks on my agenda included getting showered and dressed... Five minutes of hot steam followed by a one minute blast of ice cold, then towel off and put on the attire of the day, black t-shirt, black jeans, boots... all good.

I looked at my Rolex Submariner. It was time to get to work. I popped a Lucky Strike in my mouth and torched it with my zippo. I still carried the old stainless steel cigarette lighter from back in my days on SWAT. It has the team logo and my badge number engraved on it. The

Zippo was a gift from a cute and shapely detective lady I was seeing at the time. I'm not saying I miss the being on the police department. I'm not saying I don't. That part of my life ended when I pulled the trigger on a child molester who seemed to be *unarmed.* You know, unarmed... like the poor child that he molested was unarmed. It felt like it was like yesterday...

"Deddario, you can't do this. I got rights, asshole."

"You got rights. I got bullets. You cross a line. I cross a line. See how this works?"

I shot him in the face. According to my calculations, that's a righteous use of force.

There were consequences to my actions, a serious price to pay.

It was worth it.

Luckily, the DA in Ventura County wasn't a commie dick like that useless turd in LA County. I took a hit, but I didn't get the chair... or a lengthy sentence. Hell, I almost skated, but the local newspaper publisher was a total cop hatting ass-hat and the political pressure resulted in me doing some time. The truth be told, if they didn't send me up, the thumb-sucking, tongue clicking, busybody FBI would have gotten involved and I'd rather do a stretch in the joint than listen their candy-assed bullshit.

I was treated well during my three years in prison. I learned some new things and made some new friends.

So, to the point, I'm not a cop anymore. I'm a consultant. Although I consider myself semi-retired, I regularly take on projects for fun and profit.

What I do isn't about the money, although I'm still pissed off I was denied my pension after nineteen years on the job. But I landed on my feet a little better than anyone expected. The victim's dad in my little dead molester situation happened to be an ultra-wealthy investment banker who set me up for life. By wealthy I mean *extremely* high net worth individual. So, I'm not rich but I am as well off as I would have been had I retired after 25 years on the police department. Which is nice.

When I take on a job now, it's usually a pretty good score. All cash, no records. So, for a burned out ex-con, I'm flush financially. But this path I'm on now isn't all glamor and gravy. I spend a lot of time alone. Mostly by choice but also because a lot of people hate my guts.

This isn't a bad thing. Being a loner is a good lifestyle for me. I could have friends if I wanted, but I don't want any friends. Friends dump their drama on you. Friends are needy. Friends will walk away when you need them most. Having friends is over-rated.

Some might say I have trust issues, but I get by. Not all of the cops hate me, not all of the cons hate me, and I only do the jobs I feel like doing. I'm blessed.

I just did a quick sign of the cross after that deep thought, more from instinct than any divine inspiration. My mom was no good, but she was a loyal Catholic and raised me to be one too... more or less.

I clipped my mouse gun into the top of my Tony Lama

rough-out cowboy boot. Little Keltec .32 caliber automatics have gotten me out of a few scrapes over the years. It was small, inexpensive, and could be easily hidden, ditched, or destroyed if necessary. I kept the good stuff in the steel storage compartment bolted into the trunk of the Cadillac. By good stuff, I mean my 1911 and MP5. I also keep a healthy supply of replacement 32s in the steel box. I go through them pretty fast some days, almost like I go through ibuprofen.

Here's the thing. If I get caught with a gun they could send me back to the joint… which begs the question, how in the hell am I supposed to shoot someone if I don't have a gun? Second Amendment forever man. Stupid commie laws. I'd take my chances over the next six months and pack heat. After that, I could get my conviction expunged, carry a gun legally, and start voting Republican again. Jail focuses your politics. Ask RDJ. He gets it.

I hopped into the Cadillac and fired up the engine.

My black 1970 Deville Ragtop with its 472 cubic inch engine was a massive Detroit land yacht from an age long passed. The grateful banker gave it to me as a bonus when I got out of the state penitentiary. It fit into the lifestyle I try to maintain here in Los Angeles, the land of creeps, pervs, maggots, and of course, those other people living here… you know, the normal ones who aren't employed in the entertainment industry.

My job today is finding a missing girl, a runaway from Scranton, Pennsylvania who was unfortunately now in the hands of some Russian mobsters. It seems the Russkies intended to force her into their human trafficking racket. I considered the gig to be a recovery job. A lot like collecting money from deadbeats, which was my primary bread and butter type of gig.

The family figured out where the girl was being held via a private snoop, but the gutless Santa Monica private investigator they hired wasn't willing to retrieve her himself. He felt it was a high risk operation. So, he asked me to do the dirty work under the table. He had my name and talked them into giving him an extra twenty-five thousand dollars for contingencies, which covered my consulting fee.

It seems her daddy did well with his chain of car dealerships. I hadn't met the parents or had contact with them. Everything was being handled through the PI, who is some knob I know named Red and their lawyer, who I do not know and who has no idea I exist. I am totally off-book. I like it that way.

I scored half my fee from Red up front in cash. The PI also provided a photo of the girl and an address.

Through a couple of scouting missions and other pieces of information discreetly collected from a few confidential sources, I determined that there were up to ten guys holding the missing kid and some other girls in the house in North Pasadena that the PI had discovered. The girls were supposed to be shipped out to the Middle East where they would entertain gentlemen as modern day sex slaves. Not the pathway to film and television stardom the runaways had envisioned.

The house was in a nice residential neighborhood in North Pasadena near the Altadena town limits. This would be easy.

I grabbed some Taco Smell at the drive-through to absorb some of the residual hangover loitering in my stomach. Breakfast of champions. I didn't want to feel bloated, so I went with three Burrito Supremes and an extra-large soft drink... *mmm delicious.* I'd usually go with a six pack of tacos too but not right before a gig.

I parked my Deville in a downtown Pasadena parking structure adjacent to Colorado Street and wolfed down my nutritious bag of brunch as I prepped. I retrieved my .45 caliber Kimber Sapphire Ultra II, the MP5, and a half a dozen extra magazines for each out of trunk and put all of it in my black canvas bag. The customized 1911 had a select fire switch so I could mag-dump a dirtbag in about two seconds if I felt like wasting ammo. I shoved the gear in my big black gym bag and began the search for clean transportation.

It took a few minutes of walking around the garage before I spotted a brand new dark blue F-150 with dealer tags. No one can read, let alone remember, a dealer tag. I stole the truck. Better to take this one than swipe an older one. The owners probably haven't had the big crew cab long enough to get attached to it yet. It was new, so the victims, I mean temporary owners, would get a better insurance settlement too. Which is nice. I'm a giver.

Driving the speed limit, I headed for the residence in question. A cop buddy, who was old school and would keep his mouth shut if it meant commie maggots might get whacked, got me the rundown on my opponents. They were a pack of low level mobsters. Nobody liked them. Not even the other Russians. He hadn't heard anything about human trafficking. These turds were mostly bar bouncers and a commercial burglary crew, not that they couldn't upgrade with the proper training and mentoring.

My plan was simple. I'd go in and get the girl, then

leave. I don't like overthinking things.

As I drove the borrowed truck north across the 210 freeway, I realized I was smiling. I'm not a grim person, but I don't smile that often. Why would I? I'm not a puss. But right now, I'm definitely smiling and struggling to refrain from whistling a happy little melody. What is it about killing Russians that is so satisfying? Is it simply patriotism or do Russians just really need killing that bad? Does it even matter? Life is good and Johnny Dedd is a happy guy.

There weren't many cars on the target street. That could be good or bad. I parked a half of a block up the street from the bad guy house. I didn't want to go any farther in case I had to carry the girl. Getting any closer could get me spotted. I had no idea what shape she was in, and I knew I wasn't inclined to carry someone very far.

What if she is fat?

I pushed the thought out of my mind. She was probably not fat if she thought she could make it in Hollywood. And Russia already has an ample reserve of fat women. They wouldn't need to come here to steal more of them. I conducted some mental calculations and decided that I could carry a moderately sized woman a half-block if necessary. I did another little sign of the cross and prayed for a skinny victim to rescue. I'm not usually this religious but sometimes when you're raised Catholic you do shit like that without thinking.

There didn't seem to be any outside surveillance. A camera might be hidden in there someplace, but it didn't matter. Time to get ready.

I dug into my bag and found my Lycra neck gaiter and tugged it on over my head. I checked to make sure I didn't mess up my hair.

Don't get smart. I'm Italian, remember? I'm not vain, I just have an abundance of self-respect.

Next the paddle holster with the handgun went on my belt and the sling of the MP5 went around my neck. I put on my Ray-Ban Caravans in classic green and took one last look at myself in the rear-view mirror before the rescue.

Oh yeah, Johnny Dedd is one good looking guy.

I lingered a few more moments admiring my thick wavy hair before carefully placing a ball cap over my movie star curls. It was time to go to work.

I tugged the neck gaiter up over my face and fast walked toward the front door.

No response. So far, so good.

As I cleared the front steps, I charged the chamber of my MP5 with the ever satisfying bolt slap.

Still nothing.

I kicked the door hard and stepped into the front room.

Shit. A trip-wire.

I knew what was coming next, so I turned and sprinted balls out for the street like a pack of rabid Dobermans were nipping at my ass. I made it to mid-yard when the house exploded into a bright green and yellow flash, or what a professional demolition expert might call smithereens.

I saw my feet flying across the bright blue sky as I got tossed like a low flying turd just beyond the sidewalk and into the middle of the street. I forgot how damned hard pavement is. I sucked wind as I lay on my back involuntarily twitching like a dead frog with an electrode shoved up its butt.

My ears weren't ringing, it was more of a high pitched and painful whistle. That big bad boom was pretty loud. I about shit my pants. I didn't. But I about did.

I looked back at the house as unimaginably hot flames rolled out from the collapsing structure licking out like a lizard tongue across the front lawn. The whole house collapsed into a big pile of flat burning rubble in less than a minute.

Rat bastards were tipped off.

I didn't hear screaming. Even with my ears ringing I think I would have heard screaming, so my guess is the girls were moved. They were gone and I was set up.

Now I'm pissed off.

What a day, just as things were looking up, things turned to shit. It happens that fast sometimes. But why? What the hell was going on here?

Stupid Russians.

Note to self; *never take on a do-gooder job again. Stick with delinquent loan collections and revenge from now on... and fewer Russians. They've been a little edgy since that Eagle Rock fiasco, if that was even true. Let's hope that story never comes out.*

I finally quit twitching, laid still for a second, and sucked in a deep breath. The air was hot where I landed but not superheated and dangerous to breath... yet... but wait until the fumes from the interior furnishings roll out. Poison gas city, man.

I needed to get the hell out of there. After another moment of peaceful rest, I got enough of my bearings to sit upright. So far, so good. I slowly stood up, shaky but alive and ambulatory.

Remarkably I didn't lose my hat, so my hair still probably looks good.

I staggered over to the stolen truck, started it, and got the hell out of the Pasadena foothills. My next stop would be a drink, then I'd maybe I'd find a hotel that accepts cash payments. It was time to go underground until I figure out what just happened to Johnny Deddario's world.

CHAPTER 2

PAIN AND GAIN

After ditching the truck and picking up my Caddy, I parked behind a quiet local bar in Glendale for mental health purposes. Drinking isn't the answer to everything, but neither is yoga. Full disclosure, I don't know exactly what yoga is but I'm a fan of those pants on lady yogas, yogurts, yogettes, or whatever they call ladies who do yoga... but just the hot ones, not the ones that look like a hundred and eighty pounds of cellulite poured into a hundred pound nylon bag.

But back to the point, cocktails are the answer to my immediate needs. I sense that my brain isn't fully functioning yet after the explosion and fire. Things are still a little cloudy. Or should I say smokey? Liquor might help. It couldn't hurt. I had to take a tactical pause and assess my situation.

I parked my ass on a dark red vinyl bar stool. "Give me a Sky on the rocks, lime twist." Vodka should help me build up my resistance to Russian bullshit.

Now along with a sore nose, I have a distinctive ringing in my ears and an annoying smoke inhalation cough.

At the third drink it became crystal clear that the private investigator behind this little *'recovery'* was probably in on it with the Russians. I guess if a guy got killed in the rescue and all the evidence was destroyed and bodies incinerated to dust, then people would quit looking for the girls and there was no way to figure out what happened. The cops would look no further than the dead American at the scene. The PI could tell the parents, 'too bad, so sad,' And still walk away with the paycheck and probably a little cash bonus from the Siberian snow pimps. Money from commies, money from victims, and no payout to Johnny Dedd.

There was obviously a lot of accelerant in that house when the blast occurred. I'm thinking at least one or two 55 gallon drums of gasoline and two or three pickup truck loads of old newspapers to spread the flames around quickly. It burned super-hot and super-fast... technical arson terminology. Full disclosure, arson isn't my best thing. I don't really know what the hell they did in that house, but the result was hotter than a normal house fire and it burned long and sustained its intensity. Any bodies or evidence would be disintegrated. According to the news broadcast playing on the TV above the bar, the fire was still burning too hot for the fire department to make a direct approach. They just did their 'surround and drown' tactic from the street. That's their go-to PR move when they know nothing is getting saved that day.

I decided to make a quick trip to the head and make sure I still had eyebrows after the blast and to my comb my hair. I might be on the run from Russian mobsters or worse, but that's no excuse to not look my best.

I threw some cash on the bar and walked to the men's room. A quick inventory of my looks in the mirror confirmed I'm still as handsome as a matinee idol, except for the nose part. Eventually the swelling would go down. My eyebrows were intact, and my hair was perfect. I hated to quit looking at myself, but I needed to pee. I did the relief thing, took one more glance at my face in the mirror, and then walked outside. I strolled down the block to a busy car dealership and stole a used Buick. Nobody even paid attention. It was a plain looking black four door like some government knob might drive, very low profile.

It was time to go on offense. Screw laying low in a hotel. I would hunt down, interrogate, and kill that PI. It was just the right thing to do.

Santa Monica, California

I had been to the PI's office before and decided to start there. The snoop, a guy by the name of Ron 'Red' Heversom, was as you would suspect, a red-headed bum, liar, and asshole. I remember a few years ago I was watching some television cartoon show which professed that gingers had no soul. It made me laugh. But Mr. Heversom served perfectly as anecdotal evidence supporting that theory. I would not regret killing him today.

Red the private snoop did mostly workers' compensation cases. He had previous life experience as a sleezebag former insurance agent, a dirtbag failed real estate agent, and worthless failed corrections officer before getting into the snoop business as an employee and finally getting his own PI license. I would normally not associate with such a slug, but since he was an LA scumbag and I am sort of an LA scumbag, he and I operate in the same universe, the LA scumbag universe.

You see, there is a pecking order for the people of LA. At the top are the politicians, or as I like to call them, organized crime lackeys and communists. Then there are the celebrities and all the neurotic drama that comes with them. Following them in the pecking order are the cops, with LAPD at the top of the police food chain. After that comes criminals, drug dealers, hoods, misfits, deranged loners and people like me. Following that bunch of asshats, you got your street bums, hookers, and aspiring actors. At the lower rungs are unknown loser actors, unemployed musicians, and then finally the normal citizens. I like to think of the normal citizens as indentured servants, people who struggle along keeping the economy going in an inflated, over-expensive, and over-rated town full of ultra-wealthy assholes who own everything and everybody. Once in a while you will read that some celebrity has reached billionaire status. Rest assured they are working for the *real* wealth in LA. A billion is penny ante money at the top tiers of LA culture. The richest people are folks you have never heard of and never will. They control world-wide culture through media and sports... basically, the ultimate spy movie villains... I hope to kill one of them someday.

Now to be sure, not all the people existing at each rung of the ladder can be totally stereotyped, and there are a few exceptions at every level, but this pretty much sums up the caste system within the City of Angels.

Once in a while, one of us serendipitously gets popped up to the top of the list where, for at least a little while, we are big shit. It could be a lottery winner, some clown who has a viral video, or maybe an average citizen who does something exceptional like saving a puppy. But sooner or later they all get smacked back down. It's called life in the big city. I like it this way.

The 110 Freeway was a mess. The 10 wasn't much better. I hate driving to the west side. The drive is as brutal as a sandpaper colonoscopy. I fought the freeway traffic until I could start grabbing for any surface streets I could make my way to like a desperate hooker trying to swipe your wallet. I couldn't find street parking in the little coastal snob encampment we call Santa Monica. I parked a block away from his office at a coffee shop that validated. I picked up a small black coffee with cash. Outside I took a sip and then tossed it into the trash. Such is the parking situation in Santa Monica. I had an hour before

I'd get towed which was more than I needed. I could smell the salt air of the ocean, which reminded me that Red's office was curiously close to the beach for the money he made. He always dressed as elegantly as a human food stain and drove a twenty-five-year-old Toyota.

I only carried the P32 with me. If I had the chance to kill him, I'd do it at point blank and then toss the gun. I was reluctant to toss the 45, so it stayed in the trunk. Red didn't deserve to get shot with a 1911.

Some might scoff at my choice of weapon, but my cheap little mouse gun was the Enterprise Red Shirt of firearms. It wasn't for a collector's vault. It was a tool. That model had never failed me, and I'd shot a shitload of dirtbags with P32s over the years. I enjoyed a 95% kill rate with it, which is nice. I can't say that is totally accurate because I'm not good at percentages. But on one guy I whacked, I had to empty the entire magazine into him before he croaked so I just took 5% off for that. So, 95%. He had thicker skin than normal people or something.

As I crept down the hallway of his office building, I noticed a slightly ajar door. The glass on the top half of the door said 'Heversom Investigations.' The frame looked damaged as if some lowlife kicked it open at some point in its history.

I paused. This was an old building. Probably every door in the joint was kicked in at one time or another. But this was now, and the timing said I could be in some danger here. I was regretting not bringing the .45.

I needed to get into the office, but I didn't want to get blown away by the psycho with a shotgun who I just imagined was probably in there waiting to kill me. I decided to use some of the advanced hostage negotiating techniques I learned when I was a police officer.

"Hey…" I shouted at the open doorway.

Nothing.

"Hey asshole!"

Nothing. I guess there were no assholes inside. But sometimes assholes, by definition, do asshole shit and don't answer when called.

I decided to try again. "I'm only here to talk."

"unnnhhhhh."

Finally, a sound in response to my smooth negotiation skills. Was that a moan? Moans are sometimes sexy. A moan can also mean that an asshole got severely damaged in some way, presumably by a fellow asshole or multiple assholes. Or it could be a trap.

Squatting down low in the hallway, hoping if they shot at me they would shoot head high, I reached up inside the door and quickly felt around for a light switch. I found it and flipped on the standard business office demoralizing and putrid florescent overhead tubes. I did a quick peek into the room… no movement. I thought I heard another moaning sound and a little cough.

I waited another minute before using more high level negotiation tactics.

"Hey… I mean it asshole. I'm coming in there with a machine gun. You shoot at me and I will kill your ass. I'll kill all your asses."

More moaning.

I decided to assume some risk. I button-hooked inside the broken door jamb and advanced to a sidewall, weapon at the ready.

Well, shit.

It looked like someone had the same idea I did and shot Red first. The pasty skinned PI was alive, but I can't say he was going to be okay. He looked like the opposite of okay. His gut wound was emitting that stinky bowel smell.

I cleared the room and closet then checked him for weapons.

Red lay sprawled awkwardly on the floor behind his desk in a dark pool of blood. His eyes were wide. "Oh shit. Johnny Dedd... You're supposed to be... uh... dead."

"Afraid not, Red. I've never felt better." I kicked him hard in the ribs for double crossing me. I didn't kick him on the side he was shot in. I'm not a total asshole.

He grunted in agony.

I felt better already.

Next, I asked the obvious question. "What happened?"

"They took my gun, Dedd. The bastards shot me, cleaned out my safe, and took my gun. They double-crossed me."

That was a sad story. Not sad enough to make me cry though.

It was about to get sadder. Red didn't know it yet, but not only did someone shoot and rob him, he was now going to be interrogated. In the police academy they train you to use empathy when questioning someone. I went with that.

"They double-crossed *you*? What a bunch of assholes," I said, empathetically as I lit a cigarette.

"I know, right?" Red agreed.

Well what do you know… Empathy worked. We are communicating.

"Why did you set me up, Red?"

"Twenty-thousand bucks," he said without a hint of remorse in his voice.

Shit… how could I stay mad at him. I'd have probably killed *his* entire family for less than that. I don't actually know if he had a family, which is nice because I don't care.

I pressed him for more. "Who bought you?"

I took the cigarette out of my mouth and gave him a puff. I watched him exhale and blink a 'thanks' before he spoke again.

Red gave up the information. "Ivan Kuznetsov… we call him Khrushchev, because his name kind of sounds like that and it's funny."

I involuntarily snickered a little. "It *is* kind of funny." I had no idea that Red was such a funny guy.

Red tried to scoot up but failed. He was too weak. He lost a shit load of blood and there was a gaping hole in his gut, which in the medical world is considered a sign of poor health. He quickly gave up on the attempt to rise and continued wheezing out more information. "He said that he needed to make the parents go away before they caused problems. Killing them would draw a wider investigation. Faking the death of you and those girls made sense. If the cops found some parts of your body out front, they'd be happy and close the case. Not that many people like you anyway, Johnny. It was just the easy way to make this go away."

It wasn't so easy from my perspective. I asked my next question. "Where are the girls?"

"The Russian said they moved them to a warehouse in East LA. They're going to the Middle East tomorrow. At least that's what they told me."

"Where are the parents. How do I find them?"

"I never talked to them directly. They used the family lawyer... a lady lawyer... Suzanne Chen... but..."

He started to seriously fade... it was within the realm of possibility that Red might survive his wound... if a level three trauma team was prepped and standing by in the next office. Dumb ass.

He sensed he was screwed, and a self-preservation level of desperation kicked in. "How bad is it, Dedd? Get me to a doctor. I'll tell you anything."

"No problem, buddy. I already called for an ambulance; you're going to be just fine." I lied. 'Where can I find the warehouse?"

"All the information on the case is on a micro-flash drive hidden in my stapler. Take it... but get me to a doctor."

I glanced up at the desk. The office had been tossed but they overlooked the stapler. Snatching it off the desk, I opened it up. The drive was there. If Red wasn't lying about what was on it, I had what I needed to kill the commie, find the girl, and collect all the money. The day was looking up for me. For Red, not so much.

I admired his stapler hiding place. It was clever. If a stapler doesn't work, and it's not your stapler in the first place, nobody ever tries to refill them. They just walk around looking for another stapler. Not that anybody staples much these days. Clever.

In spite of my newfound admiration for Red's ability

to conceal stuff, I decided to go ahead and kill him. Business is business. Red was an acquaintance, not a friend, and he almost got me killed once today already. You know the old saying. *Try to kill me once, shame on you. Try to kill me twice, shame on me.*

I don't like small talk, so I just shot him in the face.

Bang. Lights out.

I checked to make sure I didn't get any blood spatter on me, then grabbed the ejected shell casing and the stapler. Carefully, I dug through his pockets and stole his phone and wallet. There might be something useful there. Maybe even money. I conducted a quick search of the place and found some nail clippers which he wouldn't be needing anymore and a bottle of Jack Daniels. I confiscated them in the interests of justice. I wiped my prints off the light switch and headed back to the car. Time to hunt Russians.

Long Beach, California

I needed to put some distance between me and the stench of Santa Monica. As a general rule, the further you are from the scene of a crime, the more difficult it is for anyone to do anything about it. I didn't feel like getting arrested for killing a guy who was already as good as dead. It was time to move on.

Speaking of moving, an army moves on its stomach and so do I. Killing double-crossing dirtbags makes me hungry. I took the 405 down to the 710 and swung down the coast to my favorite diner in Long Beach. It's on Second Street wedged in between some retail shops. It's called the Long Beach Diner, which is easy to remember.

I parked two blocks away. I disassembled the P32. I could see three sidewalk trash cans and an alley that probably had a dumpster in it between me and the diner. I didn't see any trash picking street bums on the block, not that it would matter much if they dug up a part and got their grubby fingerprints all over it. As I meandered over to the diner I subtly tossed a piece of gun in each receptacle.

The counterman sort of knew me. He always called me Senor Dedd. I called him 'Bub.' I don't know his name. I call everybody Bub. I would have to give Bub a big tip so he would recall later that I was at his place and not Santa Monica in case I needed an alibi. I ordered up a burger, fries, and a slice of pie... for my beverage I selected black coffee... I might need the caffeine boost today.

"Hey Bub, what is today, the 26th?" I asked, planting that seed of memory in his brain in case the cops talked to him.

Si, Senor Dedd... Thursday the 26th."

"Crap. I got to pay the rent on my apartment today or they'll throw my ass out on the street. Like kicking a can to the curb. That would be bad... Nobody wants to see Johnny Dedd evicted, right?"

I laid that little story in his brain that he could visualize. He would remember a can being kicked to the curb because he clearly knew what a can and a curb was. He heard my name. He heard evicted. Now I was going to make him say it.

"You don't want to see me kicked to the curb like a can, do you?"

"No, senor Dedd," he laughed. "I would not like that."

Perfect execution of a neuro-pathic linguistic technique... I Jedi-mind-hosed him, or whatever it is a Jedi does.

Obviously, I was lying about the rent but if the cops tried to pin us down, I'd just tell them I was confused. It didn't matter, Bub would remember I was in the joint on the 26th. I knew there wouldn't be a cash register tab if I handed him a twenty and told him to keep the change. That shit would go right in his pocket, so he didn't have to give any to Uncle Sam. I felt good that there wouldn't be any kind of a time stamp for them to nail me with. He would claim he lost it. I could argue that it was ridiculous to think I killed a guy in Santa Monica when I was eating lunch in Long Beach.

I could prove I was there on the 26th and they couldn't prove *exactly* what time I was there. All good so far. I'm covered.

FYI, the burger was delicious… Bub chops up his own pickle slices and uses fresh tomatoes. Not that crap the fast food burger joints use. Bub uses real food. I love that guy, whatever his real name is.

I took another big bite then tried to open Red's phone as I chewed. Red wasn't smart. I figured the passcode would be something a stupid guy would remember, his name and job. I tried the passcode RedPI and it opened up first try. Dumbass.

The phone wasn't a Cupertino special; it was the other operating system. I could open the flash drive using its little drive port. The flash device just had some information on the victim's family, the stub of the down payment, a file on the Kuznetsov guy, and a couple of pictures of the girl.

I went through the call log next. There was a lot there. I pulled the little mole notebook out of my pocket and took notes. I wondered why they called them mole notebooks. Maybe they're made out of mole hide. It seems like it would take a lot of them. Moles aren't very big. They kind of look like micro-possums. Okay, I'll get real candid here. I've never actually seen a mole. I hope I never do. They creep me out.

I found ten calls made in the last 24 hours. I wish Red was here to ask him about them. Too bad he died. Shit happens.

Call number one was repeated six times. That sounded like a possible co-conspirator. I'd check it first. The number wasn't associated with a name in his contact files so all I had was a number. I used my own smart phone to dial up a dear friend at the Ventura County Sheriff's Department while I ate a French fry drenched in catsup. We worked vice together many moons ago. A partnership in that kind of unit creates a bond between detectives that lasts a lifetime. The brotherhood established from working those kinds of specialized assignments together is unbreakable. I'm pretty sure, if necessary, Getling would take a bullet for me.

Three rings and a click later I heard a voice come on the line.

"Officer Getling." He said professionally, like a cop who means business.

"That sounds awfully formal. It's Deddario, old buddy. How you been."

"Go fuck yourself, asshole."

This is awkward.

I faked it for anyone listening at the counter. "Yeah, I'm fine... no worries... all good."

"What do you want, you worthless prick?"

I turned and lowered my voice. "I need you to run a phone number, Getling. It's important. Maybe organized crime."

"Why would I do shit for you? You boinked my ex-wife in my own house while I was passed out on the couch."

"Well, 'ex-wife' is an important distinction."

"She's an ex thanks to you... she wasn't when you boinked her.

"I was passed out on your couch too. She started it. I didn't even enjoy it."

"Bullshit."

"Maybe a little."

I don't think the quality of the boinking was the issue he was specifically calling a bullshit on.

Getling wouldn't let it go, "You should have had better judgement."

"We were all doing shots together and playing Strip Twister. What did you think was going to happen? Look Getling, if you would quit marrying exotic dancers you met at gentlemen's clubs these embarrassing kinds of things wouldn't happen. That whole mess was really your fault if you think about it."

He didn't think about it. He accused me of more shit.

"You stole my dog."

"Borrowed."

"You gave it to your girlfriend as a birthday present."

"I'm a giver."

"No, you're a liar, thief, and dirtbag. Did I mention I hate your guts?"

I faked some sincere contrition. "So, uh... I admit that whole incident was not my best moment. Mistakes were made by all parties." I paused for a moment to let that sink in before continuing. "But I missed you a lot, pal. Why, just the other day I was talking to a buddy about you. Remember that time you screwed up your back water skiing and claimed an industrial injury? I wrote a statement saying you tripped over a crack head during a drug raid and you took six months off. I mean, it was a long time ago but as it turns out, there isn't a statute of limitations on shit like that. Those were great times partner. Great times. Did I mention that the buddy I was talking to is a newspaper reporter who works public corruption stories? He was fascinated, wanted to hear every little detail. I didn't give him your name... yet."

"You dick!"

"Maybe I am a dick, but you are going to run the phone number." I raised the tension in my voice to let him know I was serious. "Do it now."

"Give me the number and then get out of my life forever, convict."

I felt that him calling me a convict was a little harsh, but I was interested in getting information, not validating my hurt feelings. I gave him the number, patiently waited on hold while he checked it, and in less than a minute I had a name.

Getling's voice was almost robotic at first. "It's registered to an Ivan Kuznetsov."

"Bingo." I was a little surprised the Russian's phone was in his own name. I guess it's my lucky day.

Getling spoke up again, "You know that kind of sounds like Khrushchev."

He snickered a little after making that observation. The way Red told it was funnier.

I focused on business, which is a common trait shared by many successful people. "Where?"

Getling gave me an address in Rancho Cucamonga... Not exactly Russian country over there. I could get up to Rancho before rush hour if I split immediately. But there was something else to say first. I took a deep breath and decided it was time to make things right with my former partner. "Thanks, Getling... look, I'm sorry about what happened. I was wrong... I was going through some shit. I'm sorry."

Getling wasn't in the accepting mood and he rejected my sincere apology outright. "Sorry asshole. This is too big to let go of."

"Yeah, that's what your wife said."

Getling is a dick.

I thought I could hear some swearing on the line as I disconnected. The phone must have picked up somebody else's call. These cell towers are notorious for cross-call interference in L.A.

For a moment I felt sad. Getling might be the closest thing I had to a friend. But having friends is overrated, so... meh. I can always rent a friend.

I finished eating, settled the tab, pulled the flash drive and sim card out of the phone, and walked back to my car. I stomped the phone flat and tossed it in the trash on the way. I opened the trunk and retrieved another P32, I keep a half a dozen of them in there alongside my quality guns. I stashed the drive in the little plastic ammo box I keep in the trunk for storing miscellaneous shit.

I drove to Rancho, figuring it was the best lead I had. I was beginning to think that maybe Ivan was a very shitty criminal. Why wouldn't he use a burner phone like a real Russian mafia player? He must have worked for the Moscow Post Office instead of the KGB like the rest of his peers.

The drive out of the west side wasn't that bad. The freeways were crowded but still flowing in my direction. I weaved through traffic, smoked some cigarettes, and listened to the local AM talk radio jocks call the mayor names. They were right. The mayor of LA is a shit weasel. I wouldn't mind kicking him in the nuts someday. I probably won't but you never know, anything can happen in Tinseltown, the happiest place on earth… or was that the mouse shop in Anaheim? Didn't matter, the general concept was correct. Kicking that commie maggot square in the gonads would be a pleasure. I allowed my mind to enjoy the fantasy of drop kicking him in the balls for a little while as I zombie drove my way to Rancho Cucamonga.

To my left, in the distance, I could see snow on the tops of the San Gabriel peaks, but it was hot as hell on the freeway. The sky was clear for a change and there was a slight breeze coming in from the west. Perfect Russian killing weather.

I needed a plan. I thought perhaps finding Ivan, beating the shit out of him, getting the location of the girls, and then killing him sounded pretty good. That is, if he was home. If I got in his house, wallet, or phone, I'd be able to figure out where the warehouse was. I'm a pretty good detective for a being an ex-convict and disgraced ex-cop. It's a gift.

Detective work isn't that hard when you have zero departmental procedures to worry about and following the stupid law isn't a requirement. Now, if internal affairs take a crack at me, I can just shoot them and bury their sorry asses in the desert… and I would too.

I was good at police shit. I liked working narcotics. I think it was the gift of gab I inherited from my mother's side. They were Sicilian… Don't tell anybody. The Bureau will open an OC case on me. Knobs…

Suddenly something else occurred to me. Everyone thinks I'm dead. Even Red thought I croaked. He won't be telling anyone I'm alive. Getling probably won't be sharing our conversation with anyone. I envisioned that poor bastard still walking around in small circles with his fist in his pocket muttering to himself like a mental patient off his meds from our last conversation. The last thing he wanted to talk about was me. Maybe I could leverage my presumed demise to my advantage.

I approached Ivan's home address and put my highway musings on hold. It was time to go to work.

CHAPTER 3

RANCHO PAIN

Rancho Cucamonga is a nice town for being mostly strip malls, shopping centers, and tract houses. If you like national chain stores you will love it there. But it is at the crossroads of a bunch of freeways and is dead center on the road to Vegas, so it has a lot of good things going for it location wise. I guess I would describe it as Phoenix an hour from the sea.

The little maggot I was looking for had a house near the old Route 66 highway in one of the tract home developments I mentioned.

Something just didn't seem right. What would a stinking Russian in the human trafficking business be doing up here? Their operation sounded like more of a Long Beach or downtown LA thing. But what I know about Russians and human trafficking could fit on a candy bar wrapper. And I don't mean those huge candy bars like we got for a quarter when I was a kid but those little tiny shits they sell now for three bucks.

The GPS on my phone got me to Rancho in good time. I sat down the street and watched. Watching is good. You get to sit quietly eat snacks and chill out. Watching is also boring. Watching is risky... How so, you ask?

Watching in a residential neighborhood puts you in risk of a Karen confrontation. You know Karens, those nasty ladies who manage the HOA, Block Watch, and the neighborhood democrat committee. Every neighborhood has a local self-appointed Queen of Sheba who deems herself the ultimate arbiter of all things and is accountable to no one. Karens have been with us throughout history and known by many names such as succubus, witch, Hillary... if you've ever been the manager, you know exactly who I mean, because she has asked to see you.

I made it through an hour of watching before the woman, a nosy busybody sporting a side-swept bob haircut with a shaved-neck short hair man-cut in the back, came out of a house and approached my car. I hate that hair style. It makes the person look like they are a woman coming and a man going, which is confusing. She was wearing black leggings and some stupid knit and glitter t-shirt top. I couldn't see her eyes behind the big dark oversized sunglasses, but I knew she was staring at me. She puffed away on a Virginia Slim like a locomotive outrunning robbers in an old black and white cowboy movie.

Dammit...

Confirmed.

A Karen.

Shit.

The woman had me in her sights. She took a few steps, assumed the slightly bent right knee with folded arm stance they all use, puffed a few more times puffs on her cigarette, and repeated, advancing approximately eight feet each time.

I tried ignoring her. It didn't work. I knew it wouldn't.

Eventually she marched over to my car and knocked on my window like it was the front door of a house.

I rolled the window down and smiled.

She talked first. "Who are you?" the thirty-to-fifty-year-old woman demanded. She defiantly flipped her expired smoke toward the street in front of my car and impatiently lit another cigarette as she waited for an answer.

It was a safe bet there was some stink-eye going on behind those glasses, I didn't say anything. I just smiled.

She began scolding me. "I'm the block watch captain here. You don't live here. I'm calling the police."

I knew immediately that she was evil incarnate, but I was ready for her. I've been fighting with these kinds of women my entire life. I have the scars to prove it.

Remaining calm, cool, and collected, I decided to join the conversation. "What's your name, miss?"

She spit it out like it meant something, "Edna St. John, block watch captain."

"May I see a badge, Captain?"

She looked confused. No one had asked her that before. "I don't carry a badge."

"Edna, may I call you Edna then?" I flashed the internationally famous Johnny Dedd smile. Women love it.

It's my superpower. The 'Karen' in this one was strong, but not powerful enough to resist my dashing grin.

She stammered a little, unsure how to answer, so I continued to pour out a generous serving of charm.

"Edna, you can see by my clothes and car, I'm not some crook. I sense we're on the same side. My business here involves a confidential financial matter. You know, courts, liens, taxes, city zoning rules."

Karens love rules. She was nibbling at the bait.

I continued with my professional-grade bullshit. "Legally, I can't discuss the details, of course. But to be fair, I think I could save one of your neighbors some embarrassment if I don't say anything further. Maybe we keep this just between you and me...with you being a captain and all. I feel as though I can trust you."

I touched the nicotine stained hand she had on my door and wiggled my eyebrows in the way only a totally handsome man like myself can do.

It worked. She squirmed a girlish squirm.

Once again, I was successfully defusing a thermonuclear Karen. It's a gift.

Block watch Edna started to light another cigarette, using her sexiest smoking technique; the old chin moving to the side, tongue flick, lip moisten, roll the cigarette in your mouth with a come hither look technique. She began raising a red plastic butane lighter with little plastic beads and some glitter glued on it to the tip of her cigarette. I slowly put my left hand on her arm this time and stopped her as I pulled my SWAT zippo out of my pocket it and lit her cigarette for her. I think that move might have totally won her over. In fact, I think at this point she was ready to hop in the car with me for a major league make-out session.

I noticed that she went through smokes pretty quickly. It was a flaw I might be able to use later.

Edna was obviously pleased a handsome man noticed how sexy she was. She blushed a little too... I think. It was difficult to be certain what was going on behind those big sunglasses of hers and the smoke cloud.

She turned her head, did a little cigarette cough, and said, "You know, sir..."

I interrupted her, "Call me Thomas," throwing out a fake name that is often used in romance novels and Hallmark Channel movies. Women love the name 'Thomas.' I don't know why. But they do.

She smiled. "Okay, Thomas. You don't have to say more. I'm way ahead of you. I knew that pushy Pearson family down the street overextended themselves when they bought that used black Navigator and went to Europe for two weeks. It's all we heard about around here for a month. Their new car, their big trip, their flashy lifestyle. I knew there was something wrong." The Karen sneered at a house down the block like it was full of Nazi collaborators.

I went with it. "Uh, I believe it's the house next door to the Pearson home, with the driveway just beyond their Navigator. The people who live there are the Pearson family's best friends. I wouldn't be surprised to find out they're all in on 'it' together."

I used her hatred of the poor Pearson family, who were probably lovely people, to my advantage, creating a fake relationship between her target and mine. "Those people," I paused and slowly shook my head in faux disgust, "they just moved in. They're from Oklahoma or Arkansas... I don't remember which, but one of those places.

"Oklahoma?" She made a face like Oklahoma was disgusting, which was totally uncalled for, but for now, we'll go with it. I love Oklahoma, especially that song about it which was made famous by the beloved Italian opera singer Luciano Pavarotti.

I continued selling my act. "I'll be completely candid, Edna. I think they plan on running a business out of their garage selling sex toys and pornography right here in the neighborhood. You know what that leads to, right?

"Egad!" Her eyes almost popped out of her head.

I thought she was going to faint. I patted her hand like I was concerned. And also, who still says *egad*?

"Why I never!" she exclaimed, although I suspected she might have.

"Do you have a card, Edna? I might need to get some more information. Perhaps over a glass of wine next week."

"Let me write it down for you, Thomas." She eagerly pulled a little pad of paper and a pencil out of somewhere. I think she must take notes as she engages in enforcing HOA rules and other busybody tasks all day. "You know, I'm married, but my husband travels and I could probably get away for a glass of wine... or whatever." She lit another cigarette and gave me a conspiratorial wink.

I took the piece of paper with the phone number. "I'll be looking forward to it Edna." I flashed my certified woman-swooning smile. "Now for our safety, I must insist you go back home. I'll call you later. Tomorrow, perhaps? Sooner if I possibly can."

"Absolutely. It's so nice to meet you, Thomas. Thank you for your service."

She winked and wiggled her hefty butt all the way back home, providing a free show that I had no interest in seeing. I had no idea what service she was thanking me for. I supposed I could l let my imagine run wild.

With the Karen appeased, I could return to watching my designated communist. So far, I sensed that the Russian wasn't home. He was probably out doing Russian shit.

Twenty minutes later, I was proven correct. I observed an ugly brown Camry wheel down the street and park in the driveway of the target's house. A rumpled dirtbag got out, an ugly man with no neck and a shaved head, a total goon.

This must be my guy.

The goon waddled into the house with his head on a swivel. He looked guilty as hell of terrible crimes, including fashion crimes. He wore a sport coat that looked like it was made out of the upholstery from my grandma's 1940's floral couch. His pants were baggy, and his loud shirt discovered a way to appear gaudier than all the fake jewelry hanging around his neck. He had his shirt half open exposing patches of hair, some patches gray, some patches dark, some patches hairless, with the gold neck chains draped about the inconsistently hairy mess. He had chest hair from hell... I'd never seen anything quite like it except on coyotes with mange.

I should probably do the world a favor and just shoot this dickhead.

I turned the key, started the engine and slowly cruised by the house, stopping a few doors down on the other side.

I got the P32 out. I wouldn't waste a 45 round or use my new 9mm on this dirtbag. I walked up, banged on the door and waited off to the side.

A gravelly voice grunted from inside with a heavy Russian accent and poor syntax, "Who it is there?"

"It's your old pal Millard Filmore."

"Who?"

"Millard Filmore from the HOA."

He opened the door a few inches and peeked out.

I stuck my gun in the opening and shot him in the nuts.

Now you can argue ballistics all day long, criticize the 32 ACP stopping power, bitch about the deficiencies of the 22LR, or even curse the 380 ACP. But don't try bitching to me about them until after some asshole shoots you in the testicles with one of these puppies. You might even call them robust at that point. Mouse gun or hand cannon, it's all about shot placement.

Kuznetsov went cross-eyed, grabbed his crotch, and fell backwards on the floor. He did not look well.

I stepped inside. "Thanks, I don't mind if I do come in for a spell... You're too kind."

Kuznetsov wasn't completely done getting his ass kicked. I saw him reaching down towards his ankle for what I supposed was a knife or gun.

Stepping deftly to the side, I kicked him in the head, quickly shuffle stepped left, then stomped on his ankle, breaking it. The little revolver in the ankle holster acted as a fulcrum making a nasty snapping sound as bones cracked and ligaments snapped.

He yipped like a bee stung puppy.

I didn't have a lot of time, so I knee-dropped with all my weight onto the center of his chest, stuck my gun barrel in his face, and made a simple inquiry.

"Where is the warehouse with the girls?"

I had always heard that Russian mobsters were tough. Maybe he wasn't a very good Russian mobster, because he started spilling his guts immediately. Unfortunately, with that thick accent and broken English, I couldn't understand what the dumbass was saying.

I started speaking in small chunks, hoping he would answer in kind. "Girls. Where?"

"City of Industry," he grunted.

His voice sounded familiar. I realized he sounded like Boris Baddenof from the cartoons.

Cool.

I pressed further. "Address?"

Nothing. He was trying to tune me out.

I shot him in the leg.

He felt it.

"Address?"

The *now* cooperative commie spit out an address. I used my finger dipped in his blood to write a report of his statement on the floor beside us so I wouldn't forget.

"Are you sure?"

"Da!"

He was sure.

I was sure.

I shot him in the eye.

The address he gave me was familiar, a massive industrial complex and storage facility combination. I recalled reading a newspaper story about a shootout with gangsters at that place a couple of years ago. A cop was wounded. Rumors suggested a kidnapped movie star was part of it. Small world.

I got up from the dead commie and looked for a piece of paper and a pencil so I could more permanently document the information he told me in a way that was more transportable than my finger painting in blood notes.

I found what I was looking for, transcribed my report, and considered the next steps as I retrieved my shell casings. I also confiscated any identifying paperwork the dead commie had laying around, his wallet, phone, and a small notebook computer. I found a leather valise on the dresser of his bedroom, so I threw all that crap in it to take with me. He kept a bottle of good vodka on the bedstand. I took that too.

The house had gas lines. I decided to break the one behind the stove. I heard the satisfying hiss of flammable gas escaping the broken copper tube.

The Karen had seen my face. I'd have to do some clean up. First things first. I wiped any prints I might have left. Tossed a throw rug from the kitchen over the blood pool. I backed the dead guy's car into the garage, put him in the trunk, then drove the car a few blocks away to a mall parking lot. I did the print wipe thing again and enjoyed a leisurely ten minute walk back to my car. I hopped in my stolen wheels, and slowly drove out of the immediate neighborhood. I made a quick turn and parked in a corner convenience store parking lot.

If things worked out, the shopping mall security would have Kuznetsov's car towed to an impound lot before it started stinking too much. If nobody checked the trunk, the car might go to a storage yard somewhere for eternity or until it got sent to a recycling company and crushed... unless someone inventoried it... which they wouldn't unless the cops got involved. Maybe, if the body was discovered, they wouldn't connect the dead communist to his house for a while, perhaps never. Worst case scenario the authorities get involved right away, in which case they'll blame it on other Russians and throw the report in the sludge pile of cases no one gives a shit about.

Getling, who got me the address, wouldn't say shit because he'd probably never hear about this little adventure. A gas line explosion wouldn't make more than a passing mention at the Los Angeles radio stations and would be totally ignored by local TV. The Times would bury it on page nine, section B. Ventura County has its own problems. Riverside County was too far away to care about.

The world can be very predictable. It's funny how Orange, Riverside, LA, and Ventura counties each act like their own separate kingdom.

I dug out my phone number for the Karen.

I heard a raspy voice grind out what sounded like hello.

"This is your friend Thomas."

"I wasn't expecting you so soon," she said with a satisfied little giggle.

"I wanted to tell you how much I enjoyed meeting you... and ask a small favor, you know, between professionals."

"Anything, Thomas." She cooed.

I heard the flick of her cigarette lighter as she lit another smoke.

"After I finished meeting the people at that house we talked about, I realized I left my Mont Blanc pen there. I called the people and asked them if I could pick it up, but they were leaving for the day. I told them you were the block watch Captain, and you were very, very competent at your job, so they said they would leave the front door unlocked. It will be on the kitchen table. They only ask that you don't leave the front door open because of the air conditioning. Could you do that for me?" Just to be clear, it wasn't the Pearson family. I was in the house next door... 3145... Remember, it isn't the Pearsons, but they *are* the Pearsons' best friends."

"Oh, I remember. I've seen that guy. The beady eyed little creep looks like a sex-offender."

"Well, if you can pick up the pen, I'll meet you tomorrow for that glass of wine. I'll be back in the area then."

"Not a problem. I'll go right now!"

I decided to make sure she would venture deep inside the house and stay a while. "Edna, I can't tell you to snoop around while you're in there, but I can't tell you *not* to either."

She gave me an understanding chuckle indicating 'message received.'

"Don't worry Thomas. If I see any evidence, I'll bring it to you."

"Thank you. I look forward to tomorrow night. I'll call in the morning and give you more specifics."

"I look forward to it too, Thomas. Until then."

I disconnected and went inside the convenience store to buy a cup of coffee and a donut. It was a typical Rancho Cucamonga day, heavy traffic, hot, and humid. I sat on the trunk of my car enjoying the snack. I washed down the last bite of donut with a gulp of coffee when I saw the huge yellow flash of an explosion and a cloud of black smoke arise. Whenever you mix a house full of gas with the flame from a bedazzled butane cigarette lighter, these blasts happen. Nobody knows why... science I guess. The piercing wail of sirens soon filled the air as every engine company in town abandoned their firehouse chili and porn in a rush to flex their muscles in front the neighborhood housewives as they bravely shot water at the fire from a distance.

The title of the news story tomorrow, if anyone actually did a story on this, would read 'massive gas explosion destroys house.' *That's the only way to deal with a Karen.*

I suspected that if I confessed what I did to her husband I would receive a case of beer on this date for the rest of my life.

Experiencing two explosions in one day might be a personal record. I got in the car and drove back to the City of Industry, only stopping to drop off parts of the P32 in various trash cans on my route.

Things were looking up.

CHAPTER 4

STATE THE PAIN

I figured the rest of the Russian bad guys would be somewhat unprepared with their fearless leader gone. I had to remember to make one of them say, 'get rid of moose and squirrel' before I killed them all. This gig would probably be easy and the whole thing would be wrapped up in time for a late dinner.

They say never count your chickens before they're hatched, but I don't like sayings. And, I prefer omelets to a dead fried chicken anyway. I'm counting this gig as a win.

I decided to buzz the girl's parent's attorney and report the good news. I had the number from the file I found in the stapler.

On the third ring, a lady picked up.

"Yes?"

This is John Deddario. I'm taking over your case from Ron Heversom."

"Why are you doing that? Where is Ron?"

"He quit."

"What?"

"I'll get the girl back. Same terms."

"I'm sorry but I'll have to speak to Mr. Heversom... I, uh..."

"If you can find him, good luck. He asked me to help and he has disappeared. I can tell you he is no longer living in L.A. or I would have my grubby little paws on him, and I would let you ask him yourself.

"What happened?"

"Maybe something or someone scared him off the case. I don't know. I've been helping him since the beginning... off book, behind the scenes. He subcontracted me to do the legwork for him. He seemed... nervous, perhaps uncertain. I don't think a job this hairy was in his comfort zone. He said he couldn't stick around. He offered me the file. I took it, and I think I can complete it. Do we have an agreement?"

"I don't think we have a choice."

"So, same terms. I get the girl. You come here and pick her up. Cash payment in full."

"Yes."

"I'll call you back soon."

"Wait... are you a licensed private investigator? What are your references?"

"No... I'm a free-lance troubleshooter. Like I mentioned, I work off the books. I get the job done. Everything I do remains confidential... forever... so, no references. Do you still want me on this?"

"Like I said, I don't feel as though we have a choice."

"Order your plane tickets. I'm going to pick her up tonight. I'll bring her to the passenger waiting parking lot at LAX. Bring the money."

She started to say something else, but I disconnected.

I entered the target location into the GPS on my phone. It was time to kill more Russians.

City Of Industry

Industry, as we locals refer to the City of Industry, is a 12 square mile block of factories and commercial space outside of Los Angeles. It is unique in that it only has a few hundred residents, like maybe three or four hundred. It's not part of the City of Los Angeles, it's an independent town. Industry is a great place for a mob take-over... Even China thinks so. Apparently, Chinese investors have been aggressively buying up property there. It's the no-man's-land of LA County. You can be in downtown LA in 20 minutes or in Palm Springs in a little over an hour. It seemed like it was about an hour drive to LAX. So, other than the hoods, communists, and industrial crud, it was a convenient town for the working commuters and businesspeople.

The drive was uneventful. Traffic was tolerable. The heat could be made manageable with sufficient air conditioning. But I needed more food. I pulled off an exit and grabbed a bag of drive-through crap. A couple of burgers, some french-fry like objects, and a large coke. I could eat as I drive.

I arrived a burger and a half later. I threw out the remainder of my lunch. The fries tasted like greasy paper. The fries In California have tasted like crap since the morons in Sacramento banned the toxic molecules containing all the goodness. I was pretty sure these burgers were made out of worms. That's why I couldn't finish them both off. I heard they do that now, secretly serve worm burgers. I don't know why. It seems like it would cost more to make a burger out of worms than it would to just go shoot some random cow.

I drove around the complex to try to get a feel for the place. I needed to calculate my staging area, escape routes, and choke points.

It didn't take long to find the shit-hole building in question, unfortunately it was a massive complex of storage, manufacturing, and distribution. The sign out front indicated over two-hundred commercial units. I had a unit number. That wasn't the problem.

My problem was, I didn't need was a crowd and the closest place to park was four hundred yards from my destination. The area was crawling with happy little workers.

What I was facing was a long walk down a narrow path between busy commercial buildings that was not suitable for a potential running gun battle with a pack of filthy communists. I mean it was fine for a gun battle, but not one you expected to win.

Nobody likes to walk into a hot zone without an easy way to get out either. What if the girl wasn't ambulatory? What if she was drugged? What if she liked these guys and didn't want to cooperate? That wasn't outside the realm of possibility. I couldn't wait forever. Sooner or later they would start wondering what happened to their boss. And the girls were getting moved soon too... big problem.

Maybe the wisest course of action would be to have a cocktail and come back after 5PM... or maybe two cocktails. I'd certainly earned a refreshing beverage after smoking a Russki and blowing up a Karen. I've been a busy citizen.

Since that plan made perfect sense, I drove to the hotel/resort bar by the golf course near the furthest edge of Industry. This is where many visitors to the surrounding commercial complexes stay. I'd been there before on a gig. It had a nice bar. The resort was built on a large sloping hill providing a nice view of Mount San Antonio in the distance. Nobody seemed to care that the hill was a retired toxic waste dump. In the City of Industry, toxic waste was irrelevant. The important thing to remember about this joint was they had beer and cocktails. The servers they hired were usually busty young hotties from the San Fernando Valley. I knew some of them from some collections work I did for porn companies. The girls were a big hit with the Chinese businessmen who frequented the place and the generous Chinese tips made their long commute worth it.

I tried to find the least radioactive place to park and wandered in. I found a small round table for two by the window and planted my ass in the red vinyl chair. I made eye contact with a nearby server and gave her the patented Johnny Dedd smile.

It worked.

She scurried over like she just spotted a big spender with a handful of fives at a strip club.

"What can I get for you handsome?" She asked as she leaned on the table exposing ample cleavage. I was surprised she knew my nickname.

"A top shelf tequila on the rocks, in a bucket, with a lime twist, beautiful. And if you get some spare time, I'm lonely and would love some company."

Women hate men who talk to them that way unless they guy is really good looking. Then it's a different set of rules.

"We'll see." She gave me a naughty wink and scampered off to submit the order to the bartender.

The bartender was a sleazy looking dude. If I had to sum him up in just one word, that word would be worthless scumbag maggot. Wait, that's three words... just pick one. You know the kind of dirtbag I mean though, long greasy hair pulled into some half-assed 1980s ponytail... a bunch of fake gold and gaudy rings... A neck tattoo of a rooster, or maybe a dolphin, it was vague... a perpetual sneer of disgust on his face... all rightfully appropriate for a random loser who is bartending in a City of Industry hotel. But I like him better than a communist. He wasn't a stranger. We'd met.

He spotted me. Sooner or later I knew he would.

He signaled to the cast of sophisticates perched at the bar with an index finger pointing at their glasses and muttered. "I'm going on break." He quickly poured each of them a complimentary shot of vodka as a gesture of appreciation for their understanding. "These are on the house. I'll be back soon."

There were no objections.

The cute waitress dropped off my cocktail and brushed her hand on my shoulder as she turned to walk away, delivering a gentle squeeze. She kept her hand there long enough to let me know that intimacy was okay between us, then hustled across the room to check on a nervous guy who was holding his hand up like he was the school nerd who knew all the test questions.

Sleazy dude waited until she was gone then parked his ass on the other chair at my table. "What are you doing here, Dedd?"

"Vacation."

My cutting humor made him snicker. I'm a funny guy.

The bartender leaned back in his seat, lifting the front two legs of his chair off the floor. "Yeah, you and half of China. What's it been?" He kind of rocked in an even rhythm as we talked.

I shrugged. "Eight years? I'm surprised you remembered."

"I always remember somebody shooting me."

"That? Wow... aren't you the sensitive little puss." For some reason, he didn't laugh at that joke.

"I was in the hospital for six months, Dedd."

"I hear the level of care in the prison hospitals is excellent."

"Oh yeah, and about the prison part... I wasn't *that* guilty."

"You were guilty enough. And you brought a handgun to a shotgun fight. What the hell did you think was going to happen?"

"You fight with what you got."

He seemed to be getting himself worked up a little. But he had a point.

"Lighten up. I put a number 4 shot load in instead of a slug or double ought... because I like you.... Be glad you're not dead."

"You're not a cop anymore, Deddario. You're just an ex-convict asshole like me now."

"I'd like to think I'm a much better asshole than you, slick... and to be perfectly honest. I forgot your name."

That was a shitty thing to say. It made him feel like I didn't care that I shot him in the ass while he was running away from a botched armed robbery. But he was right, I was an asshole now, not a cop... which has its benefits and drawbacks. The benefit was that if I decided to beat his ass, there would be no police review board. The drawback was if I decided to beat his ass, I might get arrested.

"The name is Fred Herst, you prick."

"Fred Herst You Prick... that's a funny name." I plucked a toothpick out of a little glass thingy on the table and began working on a piece of lunch stuck between a premolar and a canine... I had a dentist appointment last week, so I remember him saying those words... I'm not sure which teeth were having the sesame seed issue, but it could be those. My feigned disinterest riled him up again.

"Don't hand me any of your bullshit, Deddario... I'm here with a deal, not to rehash our past."

I have to admit, I didn't see that coming. But LA County is the home of wheelers and dealers, a magical place where you can shoot a guy in the ass and still make a deal later. It's a beautiful thing if you think about it.

"What kind of deal?"

"A collection gig, your bread and butter, Dedd. The recovery fee is half the money."

"How much?"

"We'd be getting a hundred grand for our share... fifty-fifty split. You walk away with fifty grand."

"I like the numbers, Fred Herst you prick..."

He didn't laugh. In fact, he ignored the reprise of my

hilarious earlier joke and continued, "It involves some gentlemen from Red China."

"I call them democrats. It's less racist."

He didn't get the joke. I don't think Fred follows the political news.

Fred continued, "They owe for a shipment of whores, and they stiffed the crew who sold them."

What the fuck is this? Human trafficking day? I usually get jobs retrieving gambling money or once in a while, embezzled funds and fraudulent investment bucks… I hate human trafficking. I'm not a cop, but I am a human being more or less.

"Why don't you just do it, yourself?" I asked.

"Because I like living. I'm a bartender, not a ninja, or whatever the hell you are."

"Ninja works, who's the client?"

"Are you in?"

"Sure… a job is a job. In this economy, you never know when the market will crash or boom, so you got to make money where you can."

Fred wasn't impressed with my financial know-how. He kept jabbering on.

"Look, I'll tell you, but this is between you and me."

"Just say it, I have another gig to take care of. I can't wait here all day." I was lying. I could wait there until dark before I needed to move on.

"It's the cartel."

"Bullshit, they do their own enforcement."

"Not this time. The pressure is on them right now. They're all getting rounded up and deported."

"So, a cartel guy offers this gig to a bartender? Seems a little hard to believe."

"Full disclosure, Dedd. My new wife is a niece to a major cartel guy. They're throwing me a bone. It's like a wedding present."

"Nice."

"They think I'm a pussy."

"Yeah... I sort of think that too."

"They want me to prove myself."

"Sounds about right. What's with the new wife? I thought you were married to that fat broad."

"I was, but she ran off with a used car salesman from Fresno, so I dumped her. We weren't legally married anyway."

"Oh."

"I like my new wife better."

"Is she fat too?"

"Some... not as fat as the last one," he mused wistfully.

An asshole at the bar started grumbling about needing a drink... and then he began escalating into a loud diatribe about the poor service. It was drawing attention to me and Fred which isn't ideal. People were looking at us. I cut things short.

"Fine. I'll meet you later... we'll put a plan together and do the gig."

"How do I find you?"

"Give me your pen."

He leaned forward and let me take the pen out of his pocket. I scribbled my spare burner phone number on a napkin and handed it to him.

He jammed it into his pants pocket.

I forewarned him, "Don't call before midnight tonight."

Fred just nodded and then scurried over behind the bar to settle the noisy dickhead down.

I finished my cocktail as the sun set slowly into the Pacific Ocean, or at least into some smog.

I paid my tab and wandered out to the car. Time to rescue some bimbo and make a quick score.

CHAPTER 5

PAIN AND CONFUSION

I had it figured out. The perfect parking place in which to get in and to get back out. I could easily run that distance with a fat lady over my shoulder if necessary and yet it is far enough away to allow my vehicle to be of no interest to anyone covering the target building with surveillance cameras.

I lit up a cigarette and thought about it a few moments before it was time to go in and kill everyone. I estimated that I had at least another eight hours before the stolen car I was driving became a problem. Nobody gives a shit about stolen cars. I had all my ingress and egress issues resolved. I just needed to quietly get in, grab the girl, and get out. I reviewed her photo one more time. Seventeen or eighteen, maybe nineteen... it was difficult to say for sure. White, long dark hair, very interesting pale green eyes, medium build, probably had big boobs. Nothing special about her other than the eyes. I checked the file... Jessica Swilden... what the hell kind of name is that? Total Midwesterner name. She was probably born on a farm in farmland. I respect farmers, I've just never been to a farm.

The day had been boring so far, so I decided to go ahead and have some fun. I got the MP5 out of the bag and slung the OD green canvas sling over my shoulder. I slid the 1911 into my pants, cocked and locked. The little 32 was where it always was, concealed in a cross draw configuration in a plastic inside-the-waistband holster on my left hip. I slid my black nylon neck gaiter over my head so I could cover my face during the snatch and grab in case there were surveillance cameras.

Nobody was around so I casually strolled over to the commie shop with a submachine gun in my mitts.

Just the thought of it put a little spring in my step.

At the door I paused for a second and listened... nothing. I checked the knob. It was unlocked.

Odd.

I pulled the nylon gaiter over my face, opened the door, and charged in like an idiot, or as I prefer to call it, shock and awe. A guy was standing just inside, so I kicked him in the nuts. He went down hard. As he hit the floor, a crew of four assholes came charging out of the back with guns.

I made a professional assumption that they were bad guys, so I sprayed them with the MP5. One pass left to right. Each guy caught about two rounds.

I advanced, shooting each of them in the face as I walked by, then turned and shot crushed nuts guy in the head. So far this was easier than I anticipated.

I started to go through a set of double door that the first four guys came out of. But the double doors were now filled with human flesh. A big fat, huge slob filled it. He appeared to be a very capable Russian citizen. That was bad.

The big guy, let's call him Boris, dropped back into a karate stance and then advanced in a low crouch throwing kicks and punches with his five hundred pounds of mass behind each strike. He didn't even bother using the Glock 17 stuck in a leather cross-draw holster in his waistband. It looked like the Sky Marshall model holster. But he wasn't a Sky Marshall. The airplane that could lift this big bastard hadn't been invented yet.

I backpaddled. I didn't want to shoot him and risk pissing him off. But then again, he didn't look that happy anyway.

I pulled the 45. I didn't think the 9mm submachine gun was the right weapon for the job.

The 45ACP has been around for many years. John Moses Browning, one of the founding fathers, who taught Bruce Lee Kung Fu, gave Perry Mason legal advice, and was probably the fifth Beatle, invented the Colt 45 1911 in 1904 after the venerable 38 special failed to drop doped up Moros during one of our many wars in the Pacific. Browning was not only a genius firearms designer, he was like a time-traveler, inventing the 1911 in 1904... No one had a better work ethic than John Browning... no one.

Then, after cleaning up various political, criminal, and military messes around the planet, the 1911 pistol single-handedly won back to back World Wars. The 1911 is still one of our most beloved weapons to this day. It never failed to get the job done, except maybe for the Wild Bunch but they were outnumbered 200 to 1 and had hangovers, so out an inherent sense of fairness, I don't count that one.

My 1911 was in my hand. It felt like part of my body. I knew the weapon more intimately than any lover, except not in a creepy way, just as an example of how well I know this big honking beautiful 39 ounces of God's preferred side-arm.

I pointed the barrel at Mr. Scary Big Blob Dude and pulled the trigger twice.

He wasn't impressed.

I pulled the trigger two more times, but he had his massive hands around my throat by then.

I'm going to go out on a limb here and suggest this guy was one big tough son of a bitch. He took four 240 grain jacketed hollow-points to center mass...awe shit... he's probably wearing a vest... duh. But in my defense, I didn't think they made body armor big enough to fit this turd.

With one hand around my throat he used the other to punch my favorite head.

I snap kicked him in the nuts. Nothing.

What the hell?

He pressed his body up against mine, using his full weight and digging in his legs like football players pushing the steel sled across the gridiron in training. I couldn't move my arms up to shoot him in the body or face. Mrs. Deddario's son was getting squished like a grape between Boris and the wall.

I could smell the intense stench of his stinking foul breath. It smelled like borsch.. whatever that smells like... I'll be honest with you. I don't really know what borsch smells like. But his breath stunk like a lactose intolerant possum fart. I proceeded under the assumption that the term 'possum fart' was English for borsch.

He smiled as though he had me. He knew in his heart that within seconds I'd be lying dead on the floor.

He was wrong.

My 45 had eight rounds when I started. I had already fired four. The sub gun was moshed up against my body making it useless, and as I mentioned, he held my arms down so I couldn't lift the weapon.

But he forgot something, or perhaps he simply never knew this important face about Americans. That is, we don't care. We are a resilient bunch and we don't follow convention. We are hard to kill. We hate communists, and we fight dirty.

I might be an asshole, but never doubt my patriotism.

He was holding my full weight, so I lifted my feet up off the ground as far out of the way as I could and let 4 more rounds go straight down toward the floor, firing blindly towards the vicinity of his size 14 dogs.

The big bastard wasn't wearing his bullet proof shoes today, so his eyes got wide and he let go of me when two of the rounds went through his right foot.

Paging Doctor Scholl... we have an emergency... Bring your foot repair tools stat! And some of them foam sole things.

I don't know Doctor Scholl personally, but I've been a customer for years and I think he will appreciate this referral.

I brought my knees up to my chest and kicked out, pushing him off me.

He fell on his ass, grasping at his wounded foot and whining like a dog trying to hump a porcupine.

I lifted my sub-gun and smoked the bastard.

I don't care how big you are, a half a dozen 9mm rounds in the mouth will put your ass down.

The good news was, he was down. The bad news was, five more guys just scrambled out of the back shooting. Additional good news, I had two 30 round mags clipped together. Additional bad news, the first magazine was empty... so was my 45. There wasn't time to reload. I would get my ass shot many times before I could return fire if I paused to change mags.

Technically, I believe this situation is what we in the business refer to as 'deep shit.'

Time to get creative.

I dove behind Dead Boris's body and snatched the Glock out of his holster, hoping to hell *his* magazine was topped off.

The weight of the Austrian pistol told me yes... it had a full mag so I did what any American would do in this situation, I mag-dumped the bastards.

I felt a graze along my ribs as one of the five 'new guys'

to the fight zinged me with what felt like a .380 round. I've been shot so many times over the years that I am starting to be able to discern the calibers.

My work was more effective than theirs. I mag-dumped, but with control. I took head shots after suffering the previous embarrassment of shooting Boris in his body armor.

They went down. One was still wiggling so I walked over and popped him again, as a matter of courtesy and professionalism.

I approached the door and tried to clear it using angles without giving up my position. The pie was sliced, and I moved forward.

The next room was totally empty other than a copious amount of vodka bottles, a few folding tables, and about a dozen metal folding chairs, but there was another door in the back.

I decided to take a quick break and consume a shot of vodka. It's not like these guys were going to drink it, so I don't consider stealing booze off of dead guys a crime, it was more like spoils of war. Screw it, I took a long pull off of one of the bottles.

Damn... this is good stuff. Russian-made potato whiskey... delicious.

I'd come back for the rest later.

I reloaded all my weapons, including the Glock that Boris left me in his will. He had spare magazines in his pocket, which was considerate.

The Glock seemed to be popular with the Russians. They all carried them, so I was able to collect a dozen magazines off their bodies that were compatible with the G17.

It was time to clear the next room. I expected to find a couple of dozen underage girls being held prisoner. I was only there to save one. The rest were on their own. I needed to grab Jessica and head for LAX.

I listened at the door for a moment but heard nothing.

Shit... maybe they had been moved already.

I stepped back and kicked the cheap interior door off the hinges, checked my corners, then entered carefully keeping my front site up and ready to line up on a maggot.

"What the hell?" I muttered.

One girl.

One strikingly beautiful woman naked on the floor.

Unconscious.

She was handcuffed to a big metal desk. There was a steel hoop welded to the front of the WW2 era monstrosity and one cuff was looped through it, like they do this shit all the time.

But why one girl? This was wrong... it wasn't the way it was described... except for the shit about a butt load of pissed off Russians, of course.

They roughed her up good. She was bruised and battered. That's not typical in these trafficking cases. They might drug them up, but they never damage the merchandise.

I ran back to the other room and grabbed a bottle of vodka. I yanked some clothes off of a dead guy and ripped the shirts of a few others for bandages.

I ran back and did what I could for first-aid. I took

torn strips of clothes, soaked them in vodka and wipe her wounds. I took a drink and repeated the process until she wasn't a complete mess.

I didn't uncuff her because I wasn't sure what side she was on or even who this banged up, yet magnificent specimen of womanhood might be. She looked like the girl in the photo only older.

What the hell should I do? I killed just shy of a dozen people and I have a naked lady lying here who had the living shit beat out of her.

I made an executive decision to rob the dead Russians of any money or valuables they had and to drink more vodka. I found an old grocery sack, probably left over from a supply run, and started gathering goodies. I found about three thousand bucks, some more guns, two Rolexes, an Eterna Kon Tiki Dive watch... keeping that one, and six packs of cigarettes. This was a nice little score.

I carried the bag to the back room and checked on the girl again. She was stirring.

I sat her up.

She didn't look scared, she appeared defiant. Her chin went up as she became aware of her surroundings. Her eyes were pale green, staring through me, daring me to do my worst.

I asked the twenty-five thousand dollar question. "Are you Jessica Swilden?"

She seemed confused by the question, like it had been asked and answered.

"Yes... who are you?"

I felt like she was lying but pressed on. "Your parents hired me to bring you home."

I awaited a grateful hug and squeal of delight that most of us knights in shining armor get when we save the day.

"My parents?" she asked like it was a stupid question.

"Yes."

"They both passed away three years ago."

Now it was my turn to be very confused. "So... the Russians kidnapped you to sell into slavery and... your parents are dead? Where are the other girls? Who are the people I spoke to on the phone? They checked out."

"You're an idiot... a regular Lee Harvey Oswald aren't you."

"What? Lee Harvey Oswald? What the hell are you talking about? Who are you?"

"I'm Jessica Swilden. I'm an accountant... and you're a patsy."

"You're a teenager!"

"I'm almost thirty... I just look young... Good genes."

The girl, woman, whatever, didn't seem the least bit concerned about being naked. She looked like she was nineteen or maybe twenty at the oldest. I don't know about you, but I'm starting to think this whole deal isn't what I thought it was.

There was only one more important question to ask before I grabbed my sack of goodies and did a '*didi mao*' the hell out of there. "Want a cigarette?"

He facial expression didn't change as she answered. "I'd kill for one."

At least she was cool... or maybe a killer. I gave her a smoke and lit it with my SWAT zippo. She took a long drag and let the smoke escape out of the corner of her mouth, the way women do, that suggests something without suggesting something. But she only said two words, "Nice lighter."

I wasn't moved by her compliment. Of course, it *was* a nice lighter. I'm a man of style. My response was to the point. "So, I wish you all the luck in the world, lady but I'm expecting a call and I have to go."

She took another puff, this time blowing the smoke down... that body language meant she was ready to deliver bad news... and she did.

"I've seen your face. You either get me out of here or I'll identify your dumb ass. You'll be dead by morning."

I considered killing her. I suspected she didn't think a man as good looking as me would kill an attractive woman for no reason... and on most days I wouldn't, but this is what we call a 'special circumstance.'

"Look lady, I'd like to help you, but I have a feeling I'm not getting paid by your fake parents or their fake lawyer. I also got a feeling that this little fiasco was a set-up and neither one of us was supposed to get out of here alive. Why should I go against my own interests and help you? Did I mention I already got blown up once today?"

She ignored my protests and complaining. Facts and information started rolling off her lips. None of what she told me was good. "You have the first part correct. My name *is* Jessica Swilden. I work... or worked rather, for an important film producer here in LA. I kept the books, both sets of them. I also saw stuff. He extorted money out of political figures with sex schemes using underage girls. I have the evidence hidden away. I was going to give it to the FBI but one of those assholes set me up. These assholes you killed...” she nodded towards the roomful of dead guys. “They work for the producer, or maybe he works for them... they tried to make me give my evidence up. I knew if I talked they’d murder me, so I held on. Some top FBI guys are in on it. Russians, Politicians, Hollywood types... all mixed up in this mess and I’m in the middle.”

Fuck that!

“Okay... good talk... I got to go...I hope this all works out.” I started to leave.

“I can pay you twenty-five thousand dollars cash, the biggest cab in fee history. Just drive me to the radio station.”

“Yeah, money isn’t everything, lady. I got other opportunities that pay just as well this shit and aren’t nearly as screwed up.

“Did I mention they all hate America?”

Oh, hell no? Those dirty bastards!

I replied to her with total disgust. “What? Hate America? Sick bastards!”

Jessica had captured my total attention. She continued talking as she set the hook. “This whole scam is foreign influence used to control Washington DC and the film producer is the lynchpin. He has a big mega-yacht he keeps in international waters. He ferries out key people on his helicopter. He keeps underage sex slaves, boys and girls, to entertain these people. It’s bad... once in a while he allows his clients to murder one for sport.”

“What? This... trafficker is your boss?” What scared

me wasn't the story she was revealing to me. What scared me was... it was totally believable.

She ignored my question and continued with her data dump, "and I think my evidence proves a foreign power is funding it." She leaned over and looked through the middle door into the next room. "These dead kidnappers strewn about lead me to believe the country in question might not have America's best interests at heart."

She had me. This woman was good. It's true I'm not a cop anymore. I guess I'm just a lowly ex-convict now, although I tend to think of myself as more of an Italian crime-fighting superhero. But the oath I took to uphold the Constitution stands... I always defended the rights of others. Well, except for some of the rights that dead child molester had which I trampled the shit out of. But I always felt like the founding fathers might put their hands in their pockets and walk away whistling if they ever got wind of that one. I can't see George Washington having a problem with smoking a dirt bag molester. But history isn't my best thing. Maybe George was more by the books than I thought.

Truth be told, even most convicts I knew from my prison stretch held some strong patriotic beliefs. At least the real men did. Perhaps not the petty dopers and assholes who didn't have the balls to be part of organized crime or violent crime like a professional robbery crew, you know, the kind that couldn't be maggots you could respect... Obviously they all needed killing, but the tough ones still loved their country. So, cop, soldier, convict... it didn't matter. Traitors can't be tolerated.

"So, what do you want?" I asked.

"Get me out of here, get me to the talk radio station

downtown, and get me on the air. Taking my evidence there and publicly airing my information is the only thing that will keep me alive."

I glanced back at my stack of dead communists, "Do you have any more heat coming down on you?"

"Possibly the FBI, the US Senate, the House of Representatives, the Governor of California, the Governor of New York, and maybe a few dozen foreign assassins."

"Is that all?"

"Oh, I forgot, the Mayor of Los Angeles, and any LAPD officers who support him, so maybe three cops."

If I remembered correctly, LAPD had about eight thousand guys. Having three of them supporting the mayor sounded like a lot.

I hate loose ends. I didn't have anything on the calendar other than perhaps the call from Fred Herst, and that was after midnight at the earliest so... I have some time to kill. This could be fun. Twenty-five grand is twenty-five grand, no matter how you count it.

I keep a cuff key on my key ring. It's a habit from my cop days. I uncuffed Jessica and handed her the clothes I took off the smallest of the guys I just murdered.

"Not great but it will get us to the car." I said.

"It's good enough. She took the light blue oxford dress shirt and pulled it on over her head without unbuttoning it, took the belt off the pants, and cinched it around her waist. The shirt tails were long giving her the appearance of having a sun dress. The shirt and belt kind of looked like a real outfit. Or it did until she pulled some Rocky commando boots off one of the bodies and put them on. Her feet were bigger than I thought they would be. Still, now that I look at her, she's kind of hot.

She gave me a funny look and spat out her next words. "Let's go, asshole."

She marched out the door.

I assumed she was talking to me. I was the only asshole still alive in the joint. She's not my favorite boss.

CHAPTER 6

PAIN FOR BRAIN

I picked up my grocery sack of goodies and followed her out. She didn't know where I parked. I saw my mystery woman outside tapping her foot impatiently like she was pissed off at me for her not knowing something. Women...

I closed the door and led the way.

I unlocked the car with the remote and opened the passenger side door for her. She acted like she expected it.

Good. She isn't a crackpot feminist.

I tossed the pilfered goodies in the trunk and hopped in behind the wheel.

"Where is the radio station?" I asked as I fired up the engine.

She gazed straight ahead as she answered. It was like

she was looking at a chess board and was thinking ten moves ahead. "First we have to pick up the evidence."

Dammit...

I metaphorically put my foot down on this shit, "That wasn't part of the deal, lady."

Full disclosure: I don't play chess. I can barely figure out checkers.

She pursed her lips, then spoke flatly. "I'll pay you another ten thousand."

"Let's go pick up the evidence first." I turned the wheels toward the exit and gunned it.

"Get to the street and turn left."

I followed her orders but still had questions. "How far?"

I didn't ask for specifics. I was just trying to build some rapport. I was pretty sure she was in love with me. After all, she *had* to notice how good looking I am.

"About forty minutes," she answered. "Got another cigarette?"

I shook one out of a pack for her. She popped it in her mouth, leaned in, and let me light it.

"That is forty minutes of exposure."

"Let's call it fifteen-thousand for the evidence recovery," she said without missing a beat.

"Who can't handle forty minutes of exposure? It's almost too easy."

She gave directions as required, until I interrupted with a human necessity. I took an exit to get some coffee. There was a fast food joint just to the left, so I pulled into the drive through.

"What are you doing?" she barked, looking really pissed off at me.

"Want coffee?" I asked.

"From here?" She looked at me like she just smelled wet dog poop on the bottom of her shoe.

"It's coffee." I stated flatly.

"It's a burger drive through... what kind of coffee do they have?"

"The kind of coffee that keeps burger flippers awake through their shift all night. I'm getting one."

"Fine, I'll take a Mocha Frappuccino."

"You speak pretty good Italian."

Why didn't she answer or respond to my joke? I'm sure she recognized that I'm Italian. It's pretty obvious. I'm a very handsome Italian.

My insecurities were interrupted by a mechanical voice from the glaringly bright plastic menu sign. It asked me something unintelligible. I assumed it was asking me what I wanted.

"Two black coffees."

I heard more words from the little speaker that I couldn't understand. Again, I assumed the words, if spoken without a heavy Latino accent filtered through what might have been a tin-can and string communication system, were 'drive forward.'

She put her hand on my arm. I kind of liked it. But although the gesture started out seeming friendly, her words were cranky.

"I asked for a Frap!" she hissed.

"And I don't care. I'll get you some extra sugar and creamers and then you can hold it out the window while we drive. It will probably get cold. I call that a combat frap. You'll be fine."

"Asshole." She crossed her arms as we lurched forward in line to the pay window. I got to the window and gave the skinny pimple kid ten bucks. He looked dismayed. Cash intimidates millennials, one of the many reasons I use it.

He handed me to cups of brown liquid substance and a little bag full of creamers and sugars.

"Give me four more creamers."

He didn't say anything. He just handed them to me. It wasn't like they were '*his*' creamers. They were the creamers of a giant corporation. And although they paid him good money for minimal labor, he hated them. Yeah, I read all that in his little puke face.

I offered one to Jessica.

She frowned but reluctantly took the coffee. We continued on to the next part of tonight's shit show.

We drove on surface streets until we reached Torrance. It took forty-four minutes. She was good at estimating travel time.

"Pull over here, cowboy." She said as she crushed her fourth borrowed cigarette into the ash tray of our stolen car.

Full disclosure, it wasn't a real ashtray, it was a cup holder. We used it as an ash tray. Kind of a dick move, I know... but that was our only option. Hopefully the owners had insurance for this heap.

"Now what?" I asked.

"I need you to go in there." She pointed at a large ranch style house that was in obvious need of a new roof. Some asshole installed solar panels that were falling off the metal frames and sliding down the roof destroying tiles. The streetlight shined on it in a way that forced you to notice. Dumb asses.

I asked Jessica, if that was her real name, what I thought was a legitimate question. "Why don't *you* go in there?"

"There is at least one goon..." she paused and did some mental calculations. "... or maybe more in there and they'll all need to be killed. I sense you are better at that sort of work than am I. Kill them all and then I'll come in."

That settles it. This lady is totally not my favorite employer.

I put the brakes on at the suggestion that I go murder random people. "Whoa... you didn't say anything about killing people. I'm just the chauffer-body guard guy on this gig."

"I'll pay five thousand per dead asshole as needed."

"What do they look like?"

I've only seen one guy before. He's Asian."

"I assumed we were killing Russians."

She didn't speak, she just dead-panned me face-to-face and mouthed the words, '*makes an ass out of you and of me.*'

I hate it when they do the old '*break down assume*'

thing. "You know, Jessica. I have the feeling you aren't telling me some things."

"Wow... you can fight *and* you're psychic. Listen cowboy, you are just hired muscle. I'll decide what you need to know and when you need to know it."

"I'm not a cowboy."

"No shit."

I didn't know how to take that. I consider myself to be a suave urbanite. Cowboys seem... uncivilized, brutal, and relentless... Seriously, what kind of person chases cows around and shoots villains in fair fights?

I required more clarification from my new boss. "So, I'm going in there to whack one or more Asian cats who are part of the human trafficking ring that took you and the other girls?"

"What other girls?"

"Uhhh...."

"And what human trafficking ring? Are you still thinking that's part of this?"

"I don't know what to think because you won't tell me jack shit."

Did that sound like whining?

She shook her head in a gesture of surrender and went through it again. "Fine. I'll say it once more and you try to remember. There are no girls, there is no trafficking ring, the Russians are the least of our problems, they're just third-rate fall guys, and this this is about political extortion."

"And you're a secretary or something..."

"CPA... I'm an accountant."

I decided to quit talking. The more I heard, the less I liked what I walked into. It also crossed my mind that she handled getting brutally beaten by professional psychopaths pretty well for an accountant. I'm not sure she is who she says she is... file that under brilliant deductions.

"Fine. I'll do it. But if there is any blowback on this, I'm doubling my fees."

"Just do it."

As I walked up to the house, I fought the annoying idea that if she was homely I would have called the cops and left when I found her. But she was hot. Hot chicks usually get you killed at some point... or worse. Then I rationalized my concerns by considering a decent payout... and, after all, we *are* killing some sort of communists I think, so... all good.

I carried my Kimber Sapphire Ultra II in my paw and had a couple of extra mags full of hollow point 45ACPs in my pocket. The 32 was in my waistband. As I walked, I reflected on buying a Thompson at some future date for these kinds of situations, even though they weigh a ton.

Quietly, I went to the rear entrance of the one story bungalow and listened. There were at least three guys in there, no more than five. Not a problem.

Using my finely honed stealth skills, I yanked open the door and charged in like a wild man. The house had an open floorplan. There were five guys seated or standing around the kitchen island. All of them were Asian. All of them looked scary. They had scary tattoos on their heads, scary suits, scary guns, and scary teeth full of gold, diamonds, steel, and other miscellaneous shit that doesn't belong on your fucking teeth.

Fortunately, I've seen a lot of scary looking maggots in my life. The whole concept has lost its edge on me. Many years ago, I learned that scary bastards bleed just like the rest of us. It was killing time.

The first scary guy took a 240 grain slug in the face before the rest could even react. I don't think they expected trouble.

The second guy took a pill to the chest and went down.

Guys three, four, and five were slow on the uptake. They finally figured out that a remarkably handsome Italian maniac was in the process of pooping in their Cheerios and they started pulling guns.

I did a very cool dive across the floor John Woo style. I rapidly fired five more rounds hitting number three in the groin, four in the belly, and five in the knee.

That took the starch out of their shorts.

The entire crew was down.

Pulling another mag out of my pocket I did a quick reload and shot everyone in the head who was still twitching, cussing, or complaining. Then I shot everyone in the head who wasn't. I like to be thorough when time allows. There is nothing worse than getting shot by a guy you thought you already killed.

Cruel?

Perhaps.

Necessary?

Yeah, the way I look at things, it was very necessary.

Was it difficult to kill those people in cold blood?

No. It was easy. My ears are ringing, which is annoying, but I am otherwise unscathed.

The rest of the house was clear. I found no one else.

I lit a cigarette. I felt like I earned that. A long drag sucking the smoke deep into my lungs was satisfying and relaxing. But my work is not over. I walked out the front door to get the broad.

Pro tip, once they insult drive through coffee, they're called a broad. It might be old school but it's true.

She was sitting in the passenger seat deep in thought.

She looked up as I closed. "Sounds like things got a little noisy. Neighbors will be calling the cops."

Everybody is a critic nowadays.

"Whatever. Get in, get your evidence and get out. We need to roll."

"No problem, cowboy."

"I'm not a cowboy."

I leaned on the fender and finished my cigarette while she jogged up to the house to retrieve the evidence. I knew the cops weren't coming. Neighbors don't call the cops over some loud bangs unless the shots are accompanied by nervous people running about screaming and the sound of squealing tires. These homes are well built. It wasn't a big deal.

Moments later she reappeared.

"Did you get it?"

"It wasn't where it was supposed to be."

"What? I just killed a buttload of guys for nothing?"

"No, I know another place. It's in the Beverly Hills. Go there next."

"Slow down. You said the evidence was here. What

makes you think it's in the Beverly Hills now?"

"A note on the counter."

"What?"

"Yeah, a note on the counter... a little sticky note. It said, 'taking the evidence to Coaster's house.'

"Who's Coaster?"

"My old boss."

"That's a stupid name."

"It's his nickname or something, he uses one name... Like Sonny Bono's ex-wife. Everyone calls him that."

"His name is Cher?" This is confusing.

She threw a kill stare at me, "Coaster. His name is Coaster... Like jet setting from coast to coast."

I remembered hearing of this dick before. He was a huge big shot in LA.

"Wait, you want to go to the most famous and powerful man's home in LA County and steal a file? I don't see that going well."

"It will if you steal it."

"What? No... Hell no!"

"Fifty grand."

"Where in the house do you think it is?"

"He has a steel cabinet in his home office he keeps stuff in. It will be there. He always puts things like that in it."

"No wall safe?"

"No. He doesn't trust the safe companies and locksmiths, so he just has a commercial grade steel file cabinet with a reinforced steel padlock on it. It's bolted to the floor... it works."

"That doesn't sound too bad. Actually smart."

"Yeah. He's not stupid."

"It would work out better if he was stupid."

"Yeah, but he's not," she countered.

"Fine, give me the directions."

I hopped in behind the wheel and we headed for the next stop on this FUBAR gig. I needed to wrap this up before Fred Herst called. Then I could start making some real money... but Jessica is hot, and Fred is a dirtbag. He might have to deal with me being a bit tardy.

CHAPTER 7

PAIN INSANE

A lot of these mansions look the same to me. They usually have expensive security but not good security. For it to be good, you have to have capable people monitoring it. Usually, after a week on the job with nothing happening, nobody gives a shit anymore and they slack off, typically sleeping through their shifts. Sometimes they just focus on the pool area where the hot chicks loiter, if having a bevy of sexy tomatoes around was the case for that client. I was counting on that here.

"You pal Coaster has a reputation as a player, right?" I asked as we drove to the new target location.

"If by reputation you mean a pervert who exploits men, women, and children sexually, then yes... he has a reputation."

By the tone of her voice, I sensed that she disapproved of her boss's lifestyle. I hoped that was the case and not some jealousy-revenge thing. Those change course quicker than a submarine hiding from a fleet of destroyers.

"So, we don't like him, right?" I asked, trying to pin down this situation a little more clearly.

"Like him?" She laughed. "He's the bottom-feeding scum of the earth. A no-account bastard who doesn't deserve to live. He's a traitor to his country... so no, we don't like him,. We despise his very existence and would like nothing more than to see him suffer in unimaginable misery for the remainder of eternity."

She really elaborated on that one. I think she meant it. Good. Having that level of hatred is useful in assuring that the client will be consistent in their pursuit of justice or whatever this is were doing. I'm going to say, probably justice.

"What does the layout look like?" I asked as I mentally envisioned stealing something from a Beverly Hills mansion.

"The house itself sets back about twenty-five yards from the street. There is an open lawn with statuary and a U-shaped driveway leading to the front door. He has a security guy posted there at all times. There is an alleyway though, with a service entrance. Nobody guards it. The back door has an electronic passcode. I can get you that far... then you need to go down the hall, take the first stairwell on the right, and make your way to the third floor where his personal office is located. It's right by an elevator. I don't recommend taking the elevator, it's glass and slow. It doesn't make a ding sound when it stops though... so there is that.

"What kind of lock is on the file cabinet?"

"A pretty good steel lock. I don't know locks. It has a key, not a combination."

"Fine. I can handle it. We need to swing by the auto parts store and pick up some things."

She shrugged and quit talking. I guess she was done.

I found an AutoSpot brand independent parts store on the way and got what I needed. We were good to go.

It would be time to get a fresh car soon. I'd keep an eye out. Maybe 'Coaster' would have a spare car available. He'd probably never miss it.

We made good time. The house was dark.

"He's supposed to be in New York tonight."

She appeared wistful as though she liked the idea of being in New York. It made me nervous.

"Good. That's a good place for him. He'll fit right in with the rest of the perverts and slobs," I opined.

"You don't like New York, cowboy?" she smiled like she said something clever, but it seemed more condescending than clever to me.

"No... I don't care for visiting New York. We get too many hustlers from there stinking up LA. We have plenty of our own assholes. We don't need them. They ruin the west. And I'm not a cowboy."

"Wow. You really are a cowboy... big tough man of the west," she taunted.

"Just an American doing his job, lady. So, blow it out

your ass."

That will teach her. But...

My tough talk didn't work because I self-sabotaged my bad-assery with a glance at her actual ass. She caught me looking. I couldn't resist checking it out. Nice ass. I'm an idiot.

All she did in response was emit a stifled giggle, although my strong words were intended to put her in her place, which was shut-the-fuck-up land.

I don't really have a problem with New York. It just pissed me off how she said it. Like she wanted to be there more than we wanted to be in LA... like LA was substandard. Stupid drive-through coffee hating broad.

"Okay... turn down here. Go dark..." She gestured with her left hand.

I notice left-handers. I'm left handed. It means your smarter than everyone else. I heard that on TV at least twice, so I know that shit's true.

"Where? Here?"

"Yeah... perfect... park it there and let's go."

We quietly exited the vehicle, I grabbed my bag of stuff,. and began our short approach down the alley to the back entrance. So far so good.

She whispered in my ear, which was kind of sexy. It turned me on a little. Women whispering in my ear trips all my switches and I was getting an involuntary reaction, which is not ideal to experience during burglaries.

Her voice was softened. Not the harsh she-bitch voice she had used before. "I'll do the keypad and then wait here. You get the evidence. It will be fine. Just be sneaky... I think you might be good at sneaky."

She surprised me with a peck on the cheek for good luck. Now I'm really feeling awkward as I try to stand there with her while keeping my lap out of sight. Her lips just brushed my cheek for a second, but it felt *really* good.

She punched in a code and I heard a clicking sound. The door lock was disabled. I went in.

"Hey cowboy, try to not trip over that thing." She whispered a little too loudly while displaying a totally evil grin.

I kept going and tried to think about baseball.

I passed by a storage room then the kitchen. The house was dark and silent on the inside. It was even larger than it seemed from the street. It felt more like a museum than a home. I saw dozen of photos of famous people on the walls. Big photos... all taken with Coaster standing in the middle. Former President and Mrs. Spooge on Dress, Former President and Mrs. Finally Proud of America, Former President and Mrs. Which Way Did They Go George... the whole crew. Every entertainer I ever heard of was on the wall... not the good ones, Dino, Frank, and Sammy, but the newer ones. I didn't see Duke there either now that I think about it... or Clint, or Kurt... just the assholes were there... all trying to get a piece of the action by sucking up to the Coaster.

Creepy.

The hallway she described was easy enough to find. It was wide, but not as wide as the main staircase. It was wood, no carpet. I remembered to step on the outside edge of each step to minimize creaking noises. I scampered up the six flights and to the floor on which the office was located. So far so good.

I ninja walked silently to the office door, again, it appearing exactly as she described, and quietly opened it . No problem.

I entered and looked around. I was alone.

I flicked on the little flashlight I bought and stuck it in my mouth. I found the steel cabinet. Sure enough, there was a big old hairy lock on that thing that would be a bear to pick. It would take too long to do even with my considerable skills. The heavy padlock was designed so bolt cutters wouldn't help either, not that I had a set.

I pulled the freon out of the bag and froze the lock then popped it with the ball peen hammer I picked up at the store with the rest of this stuff. The lock shattered and came open. I looked in the top drawer... just papers. Next drawer... movie film or something... it was film... Next drawer, dirty photos of women and even some of men. I examined them out of a sense of thoroughness... just the women photos. I'm not homophobic, I just don't get anything out of looking at some gay dude's wiener. I can't even process it... which is okay because I don't care what people do as long as they don't make me do it. I dig chicks... It's how I'm wired. So, don't be dicks about it... no pun intended.

Last drawer... I opened it... Holy Grail. The item she described was there in a clear plastic box. I grabbed it. I also saw another file with a photo. It was my new friend, Jessica. I didn't take time to read it. It was sealed in a clear plastic 8.5x11 envelope. I took it.

The last item on my agenda prior to exfiltration was my added signature specialty touch. I bought a lock like the one Jessica described when I purchased the freon and hammer. I slapped it on the filing cabinet, picked up the pieces of the lock I broke, and dumped them in my pocket. The first rule of burglary is not to let them know there *was* a burglary. This lock wouldn't pass close inspection , but with just a cursory look, things would appear to be undisturbed. This clever technique of deception always buys me some time. It was originally invented by Houdini, another handsome Italia of note.

I retraced my steps back downstairs. I was almost to the kitchen when a hand grabbed me by the back of the neck, spun me around, and put my nose in punching range. Dammit!!!

Once again, I took a harsh shot to the snot locker. My eyes involuntarily watered and boogers ran out of my nose. Good hit pal.

"Stop, I'm a good guy," I lied. It failed to deter him.

He drew back to hit me again. I cringed to the extent I could when I noticed Jessica sneaking up behind him with a massive iron skillet. She smacked the guy on the head with it generating an amazing amount of force for an accountant.

He staggered but stayed on his feet, turning to deal with her now.

As he let me go, I jumped on his back and started choking him out. At the same time, Jessica kicked him in the nuts with a soccer style kick from hell. I heard testicle meat crush under the blow like the sound of a dump truck operator driving over a plastic garbage bin. It was ugly. He fell straight back smashing me into the floor and knocking the wind out of me. I held on and maintained the choke hold until he went to sleepy town. I probably did him a favor. That nasty family jewels shot had to hurt.

"Did you get it?" she asked in a stage whisper.

"Yeah... Got it. No problem... did he seem extra big to you? He seemed kind of big to me."

She gave me the international recognized look of a perturbed impatient woman. "Fine, he's a big bastard, now go steal something of value."

"What?"

"They'll know there was a break-in now. Steal something to disguise what we're really here for.

I ran back into the living room and found a painting of some old-time lady in a bonnet that had some lights shining on it. It was small enough I could carry it easily.

I brought it to the kitchen and showed Jessica as she finished tying up the guard with an electrical cord she probably ripped off of one of the many high end appliances adorning the kitchen counters.

She glanced at it. "Nice selection. That's worth four million dollars."

"It ain't that great of a picture." Four million seemed like a lot of for this piece of shit.

She looked at me like I was a moron.

I confessed, "I don't *get* art." All I could see was a fat lady in a blue t-shirt with her head leaning on her hand.

"I'm not surprised," she said smugly.

I was a bit offended at her attitude. "You don't think I know stuff? I'm Italian. Did you ever hear of the Renaissance? We *own* that"

"Did you ever hear of Pablo Picasso?"

"I know a lot of Pablos... I live in Los Angeles."

"I think you might want to consider taking a class or something, cowboy."

"What's that supposed to mean?" I asked, ready to defend my knowledge of fine arts. I read Bronco Hammer books, which provided me with mastery over fine literature. I watch old school cartoons for classical music. If I hear an orchestra song, I can pretty much name the cartoon it was written for. Art can't be *that* hard. And why do we even still have art since the invention of the camera.

Jessica interrupted my deep thoughts and answered my question. "It means we got to get the hell out of here now."

We ran. I swear I heard her laughing.

CHAPTER 8

FAMILY PAIN

We made it to the car and left the scene of our latest felony without further incident. I know, leaving the scene without further incident sounds like a police report but remember, I was a great cop until I murdered a pervert.

Jessica seemed to change completely post-heist. She was almost human. I found that unnerving. Evil is more manageable. You know what's coming and you never get disappointed. This new Jessica was charming... and still hot.

"Get me somewhere I can use a phone in private, cowboy. I need to set up the deal."

"Fine but I got to go to work in about three hours so I can't mess around much longer. I got a gig with Fred Herst to go to tonight."

"I thought you said that was after midnight. You got three hours. You said so yourself. We're fine. You might be surprised what motivated people can do in three hours."

I was uncomfortable with the subliminal messaging I was receiving from her. Was she suggesting a romp in the hay? That is totally inconsistent with the broad I rescued from the warehouse. Something weird is going on. I don't like it. I'll stick it out for now in case there is sex involved, because it would be rude to not share the love machine that is Johnny Dedd with this beautiful specimen of womanhood, but... something is wrong.

I took her to a nearby office building lobby where I knew the night clerk. He was cool and could let her use a phone inside rather than using a phone booth that some bum probably wiped a booger on... or worse.

She ran in and made some calls and bounced back out, clearly elated and in a good mood.

Something isn't right. *No se bueno aqui*... like we say in the west... it means, I think I might be screwed here.

"One more stop, cowboy. I need to get the witness."

"Witness? Stop? What is this shit? I thought you were the witness. We are supposed to be going to the radio station."

"Don't worry about it. I'll get the money when I pick up the witness. We can take it from there and you can go see your girlfriend Fred Worst or whatever his name is."

"He's not my girlfriend, he's some guy I shot. I don't play for the other team... I dig women... women like you, for instance." I started giving her the trademark Johnny Deddario come hither look.

She slapped me.

"Focus, asshole, this is important shit!"

Okay, so now old Jessica is back. I've been punched in the nose, blown up, and face slapped today. I have no idea what's going on and Jessica is all pissed off again for reasons unknown to me. She isn't my favorite broad right now.

"Where to?"

She gave me a location in Malibu. Great. I didn't feel like driving to Malibu... but a job is a job. Dammit.

The coast drive at this time of night was beautiful. Stars, the moon, the surf on the sand, and the reflection of the whole thing on the water... breathtaking. It didn't take long to get to the house, high in the hills above the town. It had walls. It looked like the Alamo. I hoped that wasn't foreshadowing, because foreshadowing sucks.

"Pull over. This is it."

"Fine, I'll wait here."

"No, I need you to come with me. It's fine."

Somehow I didn't think it would be fine. We walked a short distance to a small side gate. She punched in a key code again and we entered. She seemed to relax as we strolled to the house.

I looked over the lay of the land. The house was massive and fortified. The back of it was on a steep cliff with a breathtaking view of the ocean. There were no neighbors to either side, just rocks. The estate, I think that's what you call these kinds of places, was built into the rocks with no easy access except from the front. I wondered if the owner planned it that way.

"Not tactical mode here?"

"No, this is friendly... it's my family's house."

Family? What family? When did she get a family? Does that mean husband?

I quit letting my thoughts run wild and focused on the situation at hand. "Do bad guys know you live here?" I asked with more than a little concern.

"Yeah, but they aren't expecting me to be here, so, let's see what happens."

I didn't feel reassured. How do accountants afford estates in Malibu? I thought only media superstars lives here. Or maybe other rich people. Probably not accountants.

Jessica punched another code at the front door, and we went in like she owned the place.

"I'm back, she shouted. A young girl, perhaps fifteen years old came out accompanied by a man who seemed vaguely familiar.

The girl squealed with glee, "Aunt Jessie... Where have you been!" She ran up and dived into Jessica's arms.

The guy grinned widely, clearly pleased to see Jessica.

What was he doing here? Where do I know him from? Is that her boyfriend? When did she get a stupid boyfriend?

Jessica swung the girl around as the guy approached

me with his hand out, a sign of peace.

"So, you are a friend of my sister?"

"Sister?" I asked. I hoped I didn't sound *too* relieved that this was her brother rather than boyfriend or baby-daddy, or whatever they call the guy a woman is boinking now.

"Yeah... You know Hollywood. All nepotism. Jessie never got involved until she finished accounting school and went to work for..."

Jessica interrupted, "That's enough, Hal... Mr. Dedd doesn't care about all those details. He's just a consultant."

Just a consultant?

I fought back for my place in the pecking order of this gig. "Yeah, I was brought on as a consultant... but now that I'm in this thing I feel like I'm part of it and I can stay for dinner if you want... I guess it would be a late dinner..." I ended my blabbering by sticking my paw out and introducing myself as I clasped hands with the brother. "Johnny Deddario... consulting, uh... investigator..." I paused and looked at Jessica, "And friend?"

She snorted and shook her head. "You're full of surprises, Johnny. I didn't think you cared."

This is getting awkward. "Yeah, well. I didn't think *you* cared, so..."

"Oh my god, you're in love with me." She laughed.

"No... not love... just like. Don't make it sound stupid. You're beautiful and I'm incredibly handsome and brave, so... it's normal."

For some reason the Hal dude started chuckling. "You

really can't quit charming the boys, Jessica. I thought accountants were supposed to be stuffy prudes."

"I am a stuffy prude, little brother. Let me handle this, okay. Is the car ready?"

"Yeah... I called James and Karl at the radio station. They're standing by for us to do the interview. Are you sure you want to go through with this?"

My ears perked up, "James and Karl? The AM radio shock jocks? I love those guys. Do you know them?" They both rudely ignored my fan-boy-like comments.

Jessica put her hand on her brother's shoulder. "Hal, you are the one blowing your career. When they find out half of Hollywood and their financiers are Chinese stooges, the crap will hit the fan. You're walking away from a ten million a year paycheck. I'll go back to Delta and disappear."

"We can't let these perverts get away with it, sis... we need to end it. I've got a hundred million stashed in accounts in the Caymans. I'll be fine."

I lit a cigarette as I listened. How would poor Hal ever get by on a lousy hundred million. If I hadn't forgotten my hanky, I would cry.

The kid gave me a dirty look.

"Smoking is gross," she scolded with her arms crossed and eyebrows furrowed.

"Shut up, hippy." I hate kids. I took a drag and blew smoke at her. She walked off in disgust.

Across the room, Jessica and Hal continued their conversation, oblivious to my hippy problem.

"I love you, Hal." Jessica gave her brother a sisterly

hug and kiss on the cheek. Brother or not, I felt like that was more than enough affection. Not that I'm jealous. I'm not.

Then things became less 'nice and happy' and a lot more 'bad and unhappy.' I'm trying to be polite here but if we were not in front of a kid I'd say things are turning to shit quick..

We all heard it at the same time. It was the arrival of bad news. A bunch of cars, probably cars full of assholes. I'm sure it looked like we were each holding our breath, like we were waiting for one of the others to jump off a metaphorical ledge into an icy river far below. No one talking, no one breathing, everyone wondering how difficult it is to turn invisible.

I broke the silence using the universal terminology of calm and control.

"Shit!"

Or maybe not so calm. I guess I said it louder than I intended. I meant to say something reassurring. I fucked it up. What can I say? I'm Italian and we are a passionate people.

Squealing tire sounds continued outside. And then, we heard even more squealing tires as big vehicles jammed their brakes and skidded to a stop on the street out front. Not a good sign.

I ran up the grand staircase high enough so I could peer out of the grand windows above the grand door. "Shit!" I announced again adding my new findings to my previous report. It was necessary to put what I was about to say next into its proper perspective. "About half of the Chinese army is here... Maybe a billion guys with guns. I count six carloads here now and more coming up the hill."

Jessica took command. "Haley, get to the safe room. Hal, I'll get the weapons room open, meet us there. Johnny, follow me, we got to gun up."

Hal started punching buttons on some kind of electronic device.

"What about the kid?" I asked, not that I cared.

"She's fine. Hal is taking care of it. We have a twelve hundred square foot bomb shelter built into the bedrock underneath the house with a bank vault door. She can hide there for two years without being in any danger."

"Maybe we should hide in there too?" I suggested, not fully appreciating why we needed to fight these guys if we had a safe house.

"Puss."

"You're a puss." I countered. I've always been fast thinking with a come-back.

She gave me the *'you're a moron'* look.

I was confused. Which is fine, I'm used to being confused. But I felt a bit uncomfortable with a horde of Chicoms with weapons visiting. It was going to be one of *those* nights. I wondered if I should try to call Fred at the bar and tell him I might be late for the next job. I'd hate to be tardy. That would be unprofessional.

I jogged after Jessica who was sprinting down the main hall of the big mansion. She suddenly stopped and ran her hand under a shelf. I don't know what that move was, but when she did it a pocket door automatically slid open. Inside the door was an armory that put most military weapon stashes to shame. A twenty-five by ten foot room with floor to ceiling guns, grenades, and even some missiles. I'm really liking Jessica now more than ever... but this seems like a lot of hardware for an accountant. How hard can keeping financial records be? Are bookkeepers violent by nature? Do they have a lot of enemies?

"Get what you need Johnny then follow me to the roof." Jessica pulled on a bullet resistant vest from a big stack of them and stuck a helmet over her beautiful hair. She grabbed an M4 and some grenades, a Desert Eagle 44 magnum, and a canvas bag of magazines for each.

"So, these guys aren't friendly right?" I asked as I gathered up as much shit as I could carry. I slung an AK over my back, picked out another 1911, and a Barretta M4 semi-automatic combat shotgun. I filled a big bag full of ammo that was so heavy I had to drag it.

"Not friendly, cowboy. Not friendly at all. Let's see what you got. We're heading for the roof. Use the east elevator." She pointed down a hall.

"I'm not a cowboy." I wasn't used to being in a house with an elevator let alone a house with elevators named after the points of a compass.

The Russians were dumbass flunkies who worked for the Chinese. The biggest producer in Hollywood worked for the Chinese. Hal and Jessica pretended to work with the Chinese. Who in the hell ain't working for the Chinese? That was the million dollar question. I personally didn't have a beef with the Chinese. I've never been to China, maybe it's a nice country. Not Italy nice, but probably okay for communists. I do hate communists though. Because I'm an American and I love freedom and shit.

Now more than ever I sensed that I was out of the loop on most of what was happening right now. I'm good with that. I'm smart enough to know that sometimes there is certain 'shit' I don't want to know, and the time for not knowing that particular 'shit' had arrived.

The elevator took us to the roof where I discovered that the mysterious siblings had stashed even more weapons and ammo, which was nice. This might be an interesting evening. Her brother came up next and closed the vault-like door behind us that provided the only access to the roof. I noticed they had some chain ladders stashed here and there so they could get down if necessary and some repelling gear for descending down the cliff side. Hal and Jessica acted like they did this shit all the time.

We gathered at the center of the roof. Jessica spoke first.

"Johnny, let me do a better introduction... I suspect that you've seen my brother Hal in movies. He has been in a lot of action films... a true movie star."

Hal sort of blushed at the compliment.

"Hal, this is Johnny. He's an ex-cop and a total bad ass. We need him."

Hal and I were in the process of shaking hands again when I interrupted. "So, Jessica, who are you?"

Somehow her face and deportment seemed completely different as she answered. This was another side of Jessica I hadn't seen yet. "Delta Force. JTF9Bravo. I'm assigned to a covert operation that includes the military, CIA, NSA, the LA Fusion Center, and one other organization we don't talk about. We are assigned to a special project for the president. Otherwise we don't exist. Our mission is to hunt down people who are out to subvert the American way of life. We find them and kill them. I'm an undercover operative. My brother, at great personal peril, is my witness. He helped me infiltrate this gang of traitors. Now China wants a piece of our ass because we took a massive dump on their plans."

"Nice."

"What?"

She looked confused.

I elaborated. "I was afraid you were an accountant. They creep me out with those green visor things.... and that armband? What's that stupid thing for? Yuck."

"I *am* a CPA. I'm also a soldier on what is possibly an illegal but certainly important assignment. I'm violating the posse comitatus act in a big way along with a bunch of other federal and international laws by taking on this gig. But our group works under the principle of '*don't get caught.*' So... here we are."

"Cool. Let's kill these guys."

She raised a finger like a schoolteacher. "*aaand?*"

"And *don't get caught.*"

"So, you're in?"

"Duh... you said these asshats hate America? A secret US government project underway? It doesn't get better than this. Did you see Rambo? Totally an Italian stud. Same thing." I gestured back in forth between me and my imaginary demonstration Rambo. I use my hands a lot. It's an important part of communication. That and yelling... gesturing and yelling. I explained, "I'm probably better looking than that actor and I'm a real-life man of action. Not a fictional character. You were probably were thinking that just now. Obviously. " I paused my verbal enthusiasm so they could talk. Because the sooner they were done talking I could talk some more. I'm pumped... this is cool.

Hal didn't appear to be convinced regarding my qualifications. "Where did you find this guy, sis?"

She gave me the recommendation of my life. "Under a rock. He's former SWAT, he's up to his ass in nefarious shit on a routine basis, and he's pure 'Made in the USA.' He'll do. He gets it."

"Good enough." Hal said, looking just minimally more convinced that I would be helpful in this forthcoming battle.

"What movies were you in, anyway Hal?" I asked.

"I'm in most of Quentin's movies."

"San Quinton? What? Prison movies? Those aren't very accurate. I know more than I like about *that* shit."

I don't think he was used to working with guys who absorb danger like surfers absorb sunscreen. It's so normal you don't give it much thought. I think Hal was more comfortable being with actors who worry about stupid stuff... like lattes, residuals, and stupid words on stupid paper... what do they call that? Oh yeah, scripts.

Hal made that actor face thing that makes him appear confused. He replied, "Never mind, Johnny. You just take the east corner and keep them from climbing that hill or coming over the wall. I'll take center. Jessie will take the west end. Shoot until the grounds level."

I thought that was a pretty cool thing to say. Maybe all movie stars aren't pussies after all. He seemed to have training. He also had a Steyr SSG 69 in his hands, which is a pretty nice piece of equipment for a non-soldier-cop-mercenary guy to have. He appeared to be very comfortable with it too. Cool. There is an above average chance that we won't be killed like animals in the first five minutes of this thing. But a blaze of glory is still a blaze, no matter how soon it arrives.

We took our positions and waited. The commies were getting organized. They were obviously military. Why we let these clowns come here is beyond me. They might be okay, but communism has no place on these shores. That philosophy is even registered in our theme song, land of the brave and home of the free... play ball.

I had a fairly clear field of fire. As I took my position I started pondering my beloved America, the land of opportunity. Yesterday I was just a bag man getting in fights in alleys with assholes trying to collect five large and now here I am helping Delta Force or somebody. Did she really say Delta Force? I wondered if she made that shit up. It didn't matter. I was enjoying myself. Rich people are fun.

I looked to my left, "Hey Hal."

"Yeah." He responded without looking at me.

He had his eyes on the Chinese guys. I prefer people look at me when I'm talking to them, but I think I can make an exception in this instance.

"Nice house."

"Thanks. I bought this for my sister with some of the cash I earned for part one and two of the movies we killed Carradine in."

Somehow it seemed like he didn't think I knew much about movies. He's wrong. I've had to rough up some movie stars for gambling debts and other bullshit over the years. And once an executive producer, whatever the hell that is, screwed some guys on a land deal and I had to shove him in front of a bus... so I'm practically an industry guy. Plus, I watched Lady in Cement, my favorite movie, about fifty times. Unfortunately, I don't know who the hell Carradine is. I couldn't let him know that.

"Great movies. A couple of the uh, best movies... good ones."

He didn't seem to give a shit about what I said because he was lining up a bad guy in his Kahles ZF84 10x42mm scope. I noticed his rifle had the ten round rotary magazine. You have to respect a guy who goes with the classics. I'm sure the communist he was about to shoot will appreciate the simple elegance of the weapon.

I had problems of my own popping up in the form of a six guy team trying to scurry up the side of the adjacent hill to get the high ground on us. Unfortunately for them, the only access to the top without using climbing gear provided no cover. They were hauling ass. I considered myself a dumbass for not picking up that Remington 700 I saw when we were in the gun room. My AK was good for a hundred yards and they were out at about ninety yards already. There is an old Italian saying my mom used to tell us when we were little, iron sights are for iron men. I quit commiserating about my weapon selections, lined up some commies, and started squeezing off rounds. Pop...Pop... Pop... Pop... Pop... Pop.

I got five out of six. Number six scrambled back down the hill though. I think he decided to find another route after the assholes in front of him got whacked.

I had a moment to relax so I lit another cigarette and

loaded up my shotgun with slugs. Might as well make a good impression on these guys. I looked over to see another side of Jessica. She was firing her M4. In the muzzle flashes I could see her still dressed in that dress shirt I took off a dead guy and those combat boots from a different dead guy. But she looked sexy as hell. Hair wild, the rest of her all legs and rage. The visual kind of turned me on. My shorts started feeling uncomfortable, so I turned my attention back to the task at hand.

Some more guys were coming over the wall. This time they used cover fire and tactical movement like professionals instead of a bunch of half-wit gangsters running in a line up a trail. I put my cigarette down and started firing my shotgun. My targets had to feel like they were suffering the wrath of an F5 Texas tornado. The first slug hit their lead guy in the throat. His head was still attached... barely. The second hit a guy in the leg below the knee. That extremity *did* fly off. Ouch. I think he decided to quit and go into the ministry or a convent or wherever it is bad guys go to repent their badness. Two others were on the ground twitching. I didn't see where I hit them, but they were sort of gooey, so I'm going with lower center mass.

I ducked as some nearly well-placed rounds danced about my hidey-hole. I scooted down a few feet. Shoot and move should be written into the Constitution. How could they forget that gem?

I popped up again and started pumping rounds at the advancing crew. I hit another one and missed one. They started peppering my position again. Shit... time to switch back to the AK. I slapped in a fresh magazine.

I moved the other direction this time and popped up

long enough to mag-dump the pack of them in an attempt to discourage their advance.

They were sufficiently discouraged. Two of them were terminally discouraged.

I reloaded and moved a few feet further down the wall. At this point I realized the walls around the rooftop were reinforced. Normal cinderblock would be coming apart by now. Sweet.

Shit... about twenty of them were swarming the perimeter I was supposed to be covering, maybe more. I could see this being a problem.

I saw movement over my shoulder and there was Jessica standing behind me with a belt-fed machine gun. Now I was totally going full speed to boner city.

She let the M-249 SAW rip and she shredded the meat socks who were bum rushing us. The ocean wind was blowing her hair, her green eyes were reflecting the flames rolling out of the barrel, and her face had the snarl of a warrior woman with blood lust turning that sneer of hate into the most kissable lips I have ever seen. I was in jeopardy of unintentionally pole-vaulting over the wall.

"Thank you, Jessica." It was the only thing I could manage to say.

"You're welcome, cowboy... Get ready, we're going to make a break for it."

"I was just having fun," I said in sort of a protesting way to cover the fact that I wasn't ready to leave my kneeling position just yet. I needed to think about baseball some more before I could get up.

"I'm going to cull their numbers some more then we're getting in the car and making a run for the radio station."

"What about the kid?"

"She'll be safer staying here in the panic room."

"Fine. I'll be ready."

I returned to shooting communists for fun and profit.

Jessica ran back to her position and did some more SAW stuff. Hal was popping off a few of their leaders who were staged along the road. Dummies. Just because you think your out of range doesn't mean you are *really* out of range. Never abandon cover or concealment, but mostly cover, except to move. And I thought we were fighting professionals... What a bunch of pukes.

Then a thought occurred to me. No cops. We were in Malibu, so the County provided law enforcement services here.

"Where's the sheriff?" I asked to no one in particular. I wasn't sure the Sheriff was prepared for this kind of fight anyway, but someone had to call by now about World War III being fought on the slopes of the mountains of Malibu. This particular location in the playground of the stars was starting to look like Pork Chop Hill.

Hal answered as he sustained fire, "Jessie had a vacant building full of ISIS paraphernalia set to explode near Gorman in the event these guys attacked here. The entire Sheriff's office is on tactical alert and heading up to the north county line. Every Deputy on the Department is busy whacking it to the idea of shooting some terrorists."

"Smart. If they are at Gorman they might as well be on Mars."

"Yeah, and all the real terrorists are down here with us."

I had to think about that. "Are communists terrorists? Or are terrorists communists...I get these things mixed up sometimes."

He didn't answer. There was movement again... the hill.

I let another three round burst rip, shooting at a clown who was trying to do the mountain path thing again. He died a sudden death. Shit happens. It happens more often when you're stupid.

What was that famous Westmorland quote? If you shoot enough of them, they'll quit fighting? Well, we just shot a shitload of them and they're still fighting. I don't think they're well read.

I popped another turkey. Soon it would be time to move out. Then things could get dangerous.

CHAPTER 9

PAIN AND BEANS

I t took us only a few minutes after getting Jessica's signal for us to get organized and rolling. For a bean counter and a thespian, Hal and Jessica were pretty good at coping with stressful situations. At this point, I still thought it was very odd for an actor and an accountant to be prepared for Chinese Army assaults, living in secret Bond villain lairs, or driving in high speed chases across Los Angeles… But remember, this is LA… so communists, super villain lairs, and car chases are an everyday way of life for us. We eat earthquakes for breakfast and fart tsunamis before lunch… or something… I'm not sure tsunami farts are a real thing so let's just agree that we all live on a jagged edge here in the land of swimming pools and movie stars, as Uncle Jed used to say.

The three of us took the north elevator this time and descended into a massive underground garage. Massive doesn't do it justice. It looked like it was big enough to host a NASCAR event.

I was instantly in awe of the dozens of beautiful vehicles in the garage, all brand new models, but strangely, no classics. I found that to be tasteless. But even without classics, there was one very interesting car that caught my eye more than the others. It was a large black Rolls Royce limousine parked at the far end. It was a beast. The thing looked as big as a city bus. Impressive.

My eyes were also drawn to a black Jaguar XJR575... The number represented its horsepower. It could hit sixty miles an hour in under four seconds. Across the rows I spotted a Mercedes-AMG GT 63S, the sedan version with a twin-turbocharged V8 engine. There were four Tesla Model S Performance electric cars in four different colors... they had some fast cars in this fleet.

We sprinted past them, gunned up and ready for action. Jessica was still rocking the SAW, I had my AK, and Hal was toting an M4 as we ran through the sprawling garage toward the big Rolls.

We got the car. I started to get in, but Jessica stopped me. "Johnny, take the Bentley and clear a path for us. We have comm links set up, so we'll be able to talk to each other. I'll guide you to the radio station. Play as rough as you need to with it. We have five more of them stored at the big house. This one is just a spare."

Big house? They had a bigger house than this? What is this thing, an emergency spare cottage?

As much as I wanted to ride with Jessica and share some quality high speed chase time with her, I decided I would rather drive a Bentley. I'd never been behind the wheel of one. Once I yanked a tech company CEO out of a Bentley and broke his arm, so that was kind of like a test drive. I remember that day distinctly because of the beautiful car. He screwed some investors and he didn't quite get how it was important to square things with them. I helped him remember. He lived through the counseling session, but now he has a speech impediment. Maybe he'd invent an app for that someday.

Focus, Johnny... this is serious.

I quit my daydreaming about cars. "Keys?" I asked.

"Keys are in it. And FYI, this one is armored up like the Presidential beast. Self-sealing tires and bullet resistant glass. You're as safe in this as a baby in your mother's arms."

Not the best analogy. My mom rode with the Hell's Angels... She gave me up for adoption, or more specifically, traded me for a Remington 870 and a case of Old Milwaukee. Her arms weren't the safest place to be when I was growing up. After I was a little older, she squared herself away and apologized. It was a special moment. Mom put her arm around me and said, "Remember when I gave you away for some beer and a gun?" I said, "yes." She looked me in the eyes and said... and I'll never forget this, "Johnny, that was a dick move. Sorry, asshole, walk it off." Mom really turned her life around after that and somehow scored a job as a prison guard in Alabama. We stay in touch. Our relationship is pretty good right now.

Enough reminiscing.

Jessica put her hand on my shoulder, which I liked.

"Johnny, you take this with you. That way if they take down our car, you can still get this to the radio station.

The commies will think you are just some disposable security. James and Karl at the radio station will know what to do with it."

She placed the small flash drive in my hand, gave me another unexpected peck on the cheek, and hopped into the rolls.

I put the drive in my pocket and jumped in behind the wheel of one of my dream cars.

The Bentley was a powerful brute. The Moroccan Blue Flying Spur model that I was driving had a 6.0 liter W12 engine that was capable of doing over two-hundred miles an hour. I read about it in one of my car magazines. This was my fantasy come true. At least my *car* fantasy. I have others that I'm not prepared to discuss publicly involving three blind strippers and a turtle... If you heard the whole thing it doesn't really sound *that* weird.

I rolled out of the garage on the twenty-two inch wheels and kicked this leather and steel hottie in the ass. She might weigh about fifty-four hundred pounds, but she was my baby tonight and my baby wanted to run.

The Chinese assassins were on my ass as we blasted out of the underground garage and onto the winding narrow hillside street skidding and squealing tires. Once we hit pavement I could see that the rat bastards had roadblocks set up with their vehicles a quarter mile up the street in both directions.

Jessica's voice came through the Naim stereo system, which had killer sound by the way, advising me to go right and up the hill.

I believe previously she mentioned something about playing rough and plowing a path.

I rolled my window down, stomped on the gas, jerked the wheel, and pulled a rolling 180... I threw the screaming car in reverse and executed a fifty mile an hour demolition derby move on their roadblock, hitting it square with my back bumper. Two of their SUVs spun into the ditch and a third went down the hill and exploded like it had been full of bombs and other nasty stuff.

They had a couple of backup guys on foot. I popped them with my 1911 as I passed at point blank range. I was close enough to see in their faces that they appeared to be reconsidering their life choices as big fat slugs travelling at 810 feet per second clocked each of them in the melon. Adios, dirtbags... or sayonara, or whatever they say in China when some asshole steps on that slick and slippery water slide to hell.

I whipped the car back around nose forward and kicked it in the ass with the limo beast right behind me.

From the stereo, I heard her say, "Nice work, cowboy." Positive reinforcement is always welcome.

Jessica's voice continued skillfully guiding me through the chaotic chase, giving me directions as we sped up and across the village streets to Malibu Canyon Road. It was about to get rodeo style out here.

The commie shitbirds got organized again after I destroyed their candy-assed roadblock and went into full aggressive pursuit mode. They couldn't afford to have their big Hollywood and Washington extortion spy ring exposed, or maybe there were some more missing girls, or Russians, or something else they were concerned about too... or not... Let me be real candid here. I'm kind of lost as to what the hell is going on. All I know is I got to finish this gig, get paid, get Jessica's phone number, and then go help that guy I used to shoot, Fred Herst You Prick, with the next job.

I pushed Fred's job out of my head and focused on my driving. The Bentley was surreal. It handled the road like Rembrandt handled a Stradivarius, eating up pavement like a cur dog eats turds, only more elegantly. I felt like a professional race car driver. When I was on the police department I was a pursuit driving instructor. We did some crazy stuff with shitty cars. Now I could get even crazier with a high-end precision performance car. I was strangely aroused. Even much more than normal strangely aroused.

In my rear view mirror, I watched as Jessica stood up through the sunroof and emptied her belt-fed machine gun into the pursuing commie cars. One of them skidded off the road and into a tree. A second one crashed into a third one, and another just slowed and stopped. It didn't have a windshield anymore and the driver appeared to be seriously dead. Only five of these butt holes left... winning!

Malibu Canyon Road can be treacherous even when many carloads of foreign assassins aren't attempting to murder you. At night, at speeds in excess of one-hundred-and-forty, and after drinking all day, some claim it can be even *more* treacherous. And also, to make things even more challenging, I do have multiple carloads of foreign assassins trying to kill me.

Fighting the wheel, I navigated a decreasing radius curve at around seventy. It felt like the tires were ripping off of the rims, but I didn't want to eat the thousand foot drop that was inches from my passenger side door.

So, here's a fair question. When a delivery truck breaks

down at night, aren't they supposed to have flares, or cones, or some shit out? Because the broken down delivery truck in front of me didn't have any of that shit. I tried to steer around the stalled brown van but in spite of my car's weight, gravity and centrifugal force saw things differently.

I hit it the delivery van an odd angle sending it over the cliff into darkness and me into a wild dust kicking spin. The Rolls tried to maneuver out of my crash but went into a side spin, then roll, then into some boulders on the inside edge of the roadway.

I cracked my head and was out cold. Somehow, I still was able to get stopped but it felt like I had two tires hanging off the side of the cliff. I must have cracked my head on the bulletproof window, which was pretty hard, because I had blood running down my face.

I was still in a state of being knocked goofy. I turned and saw the commies rush the Rolls and capture Jessica and Hal. That wasn't ideal. I guess I didn't matter because they tossed them into a blue Mercedes and disappeared back up the road towards Malibu.

I suspect they could have run up and took a look at me right after the crash and thought I was dead. Who knows? I was hurting. Maybe knocked out and didn't know it.

Today was turning into one of those days where you start to consider other career options. I could have been a mechanic, a plumber, a cook, *but noooooo*. I had to be a professional problem solver, or as some crass lowlife people refer to my profession, a bagman.

I stepped out of the Bentley. There was still a cloud of dust lingering in the air. I glanced at my Rolex. I still had a couple of hours to kill before Fred called about the cartel job.

I lit up a cigarette.

Well, shit.

CHAPTER 10

DRAIN SOME PAIN

So... do I just wait here? Or...

My path was unclear, so I smoked one more cigarette before doing a walk-around of the Bentley to assess what degree of screwed my car situation was.

It wasn't great. A few dings and bullet holes, one tire over the edge and one dangerously close to a crumbling berm and a four hundred foot drop. If I was careful and babied it with some gentle steering, I could inch the big luxury car back off the ledge and onto the road again without having it do a Greg Louganis dive off the cliffside.

That random thought initiated memories of watching the cliff divers in Acapulco who were in the King's movie he filmed there. What would Elvis do in this situation? He was a favorite of mine, a great Italian tenor and man of action. I suspected if he were in my shoes, he would get this Bentley rolling, make out with Ann Margaret, execute some air karate moves, and then go fuck up some bad guys. My path had been vague but now it is now clear. It was time to take care of business. I would rescue Jessica and kick some commie ass for America.

And her brother too... I'd totally rescue Hal or whatever his name was.

It seems like there was a kid involved. What was the deal with her? Oh yeah, safe room and video games. I have to admit. I'm not a big fan of kids. The act weird and smell funny. So, she doesn't need rescued right now and that's okay with me.

Step two... how do I rescue them? Answer: I'd do some hero stuff.

Okay most of the basics were now settled. Where were they? My guess is the Chinese intelligence operatives took them back to the house. Why else would they go in that direction unless they were lost. Asian drivers... I know, I know, we don't do stereotypes anymore... But I don't care. I lived in Irvine, California for six months. I know all about Asian drivers. Great at math, nice people, but they suck at driving. I don't know why. I don't think they know why either.

Using all my driving skills and patience, I carefully got the Bentley on Malibu Canyon Road again. I dug into my canvas bag and retrieved some ammo for the 45 and a fresh mag for the MP5. I'm taking these dirtbags down, Elvis style.

Ten minutes later I'm on the side of the road watching the mansion. I remembered our fight from earlier and how cool it was that even a platoon of trained Chinese military types couldn't take it down...It was funny then. Now, *I* got to take it down and I'm starting to think it's very sad.

I could climb the cliff, but I'm a little uncomfortable with heights and I can't climb for shit. For one thing, climbing is hard to do. For another, it makes my arms tired. Climbing a sheer rock wall like the one on the back of the property requires some equipment I don't have. But mainly, I am dismissing that approach because heights creep me out. My mild acrophobia caused me a lot of heartburn in SWAT which is why I stayed on the entry team during my tenure there. That and a turn at sniper... but... heights suck.

So, what are my options? Do I bum rush these guys and die in a hail of gunfire? Looks cool, accomplishes nothing, get seriously killed in painful ways. *nah*... screw that.

Do I drop in with a parachute? Requires an airplane, parachute, skills I don't have, and once again, heights. Oh *hell* no.

Do I go help Fred and come back later to see how all this turned out?

I'd be alive but I'd know I was a puss for the rest of my life and the commies get away with taking a dump on America's head... Forget about it. Not happening.

Wait... I'll use deception. The Trojans, who were very fine Italians and went on to invent the condom, used a wooden horse to overcome some random guys they had a beef with. But I don't have a wooden horse... Scratch deception.

I'll go with stealth.

I suspected that the Chinese guys weren't presently concerned about encroachment by enemy forces. They were focused on getting a data drive and beating the information out of Hal and Jessica to uncover what they had accomplished with their investigation, and to verify that the pair didn't reveal their findings to anyone else. This was red alert damage control time for China and for the biggest espionage operation they've launched against the US since they stole all of our space technology. The Chinese spies would be very busy communists. They would never anticipate that one of the most handsome Italian men in Los Angeles would sneak down there and launch a rescue. As far as they were concerned, the action was over. So, there would be minimal perimeter security.

I didn't completely believe that they wouldn't be on their toes, but I was going with it. I couldn't come up with any other options.

I made an approach in the darkness to a side service gate I noticed when Jessica and I arrived the first time.

Things were evolving in my favor. It was dark. The night was alive with hordes of commie bastards. I had a gun. A mysterious hot chick was in peril. I'm a studly classical Italian hero type who is as handsome as Franco Nero except for my bent nose that still hurts a little... The conditions for success were perfect.

With my 1911 in my hand, I made my way to the gate undetected, at least as far as I knew. They might have detected me and were just lining up the best sniper shot. That would suck, big time. I pushed that thought out of my mind and focused on finding Jessica. I'm sure she has a total crush on me, so it's the least I can do for her.

I got in without incident and ducked behind the garbage bins. I was surprised people in Malibu had garbage cans. I thought an environmental fairy came down from above, shoved all the rich people's garbage up its butt, and then keistered it back to heaven where it was converted to multi-colored glitter and platitudes.

How things went this well so far was amazing. I'm pretty sure they thought I was dead or at least out of action at the crash scene. Big mistake, you commie mugs.

I assessed the lawn area. A couple of guys wandering around, no rifles. That meant most of them were dispersed back to other assignments across the country, except the for the interrogation crew and an anemic security detail. They believed they already won. Hell, this shit is just getting started. I suppressed a chuckle. This is such fun.

Now the task at hand is to either neutralize the sentries or stealth past them to the house. At this point I was wishing I knew kung fu. I could do some ninja backflips, do a flying spinning back kick, and knock them both unconscious. Not that I couldn't do that, I just didn't feel like it right now.

As one guy walked around to the west side of the house, I noted that the other walked closer to me by the East side. There was an opportunity there to take at least one of them out.

I noticed that the garbage cans were sitting on patio pavers, those sixteen inch square flat things you use to make instant sidewalks. I was able to pull one up. Not all people look at a paver and think impact weapon, but I'm creative.

I creeped up on the guy.

He didn't see or hear me. He was a shitty sentry.

I lifted the paver as high above my head as my arms would reach and swung down with all of my might, decreasing the sentry's height by about eight inches. The paver broke apart on his noggin which, in turn, broke like a cracked egg. I intended to just knock him out, but a pancaked head is just as good, maybe even better. I dragged his body back to the garbage cans leaving a remarkably obvious trail of goo from the mess I made to the hiding place. I moved over behind the nearby cars and waited.

Sentry number two came by and immediately noticed a couple of very important things. One, his partner was missing, and two, there was a slime trail of brain matter and drag marks leading to the garbage cans.

He focused on the drag marks as he tactically moved towards the cans.

As he intently approached the cans, I left my hiding place by the cars and came up behind him. I gave him my bread and butter move. I swung my arm out wide and ka-whapped him on the ear with the flat side of my 1911 as hard as I could. He was clearly stunned but for some reason he didn't go down. I did it again. He went down. I did a knee drop on his neck, delivering my full weight on it. I heard the satisfying snap. When you start killing commies with your bare hands it's difficult to stop at just one... well, not just bare hands, but holding patio pavers or guns too. Any of those.

Sentry two joined sentry one behind the trash cans. I went to the house. It was time to get the girl.

The lights were off on the main floor. I went to the

servant's entrance and stealthed my way into the kitchen like a shadow ninja, which is the most dangerous kind of ninja... I guess. Full disclosure, I just made that up.

There were sounds from the sub-level of the house. They didn't sound friendly.

I decided that having the data on me might not be a great idea in case things went south. I opened a kitchen cabinet and dropped the tiny flash drive into a coffee cup on the shelf. It wasn't a perfect hiding place, but it would take forever to find it if I got killed. If nothing else, they'd be annoyed.

I closed in on the sounds... they were in the study. I always wanted a house with a study, except I hate studying. I quick peeked in.

Hal was on the floor bloodied up. Jessica was duct taped to a chair and had been slapped around a little. A half-dozen dirtbags were taking turns kicking Hal and being dicks. An older guy was zapping Jessica with an electronic weapon like the police use. She was defiant, but I don't think she appreciated the sadistic shocks to the private parts this maggot was delivering.

So far, I think it's safe to say nobody talked yet. But from the look of the scene, there wasn't much chance of the bad guys letting Jessica and Hal leave the place alive.

I found myself wishing I had some help. I thought about calling a prison buddy named Gunther Fuques, but he was in Long Beach and it would take too long for him to get there. He was a tough bastard. I could use his assistance. I guess that was the only guy I knew who would help. I have no friends to speak of.

I decided I needed to get some leverage before engaging these assholes. I backed away and creeped up the stairs to the next floor. There was a guy in Hal's home office searching the place. How did I know this was Hal's home office? I was a highly trained law enforcement investigator. I observed that one of the walls of the room had a painting of him with that kid I almost forgot about again. I noticed a couple of bottles of expensive gin on a rolling bar and I suspect that actors drink a lot of gin. There were some trophies for being good at pretending adorning the bookcase. Also, he had a little metal sign on the desk that had 'Hal's Home Office' with a screwy looking happy face thing engraved on it. It was like a pair of deflated happy faces. One was laughing and one was crying... creepy... When you think about it, Hal must be one sick fuck. Most actors are.

The jerk who was searching the place had his back to me, so I came up behind him and smacked his melon with the flat side of the 45. He was stunned. I spun him around and gave him my patented reverse karate chop to the balls and an elbow to the temple. Then, when he fell to the ground, I strangled him with his necktie. I hate neckties. I hate bad guys. I hate everything.

Okay, I was a little wound up. I felt myself going full psycho there for a moment. Killing people with your bare hands does that to you sometimes. I don't know why. All is calm now.

Suddenly a wave of realization came over me. Shit. I meant to take him prisoner and I killed him. Why do I keep doing that?

I'd find another one.

I went down a hall and found another loser searching a bedroom. I didn't analyze it. I just walked up behind him and punched him in the back of the head as hard as I could. It worked. He sagged. I grabbed him.

I got him ambulatory and marched him down the stairs with my gun screwed in his ear. Once again, my plans were working perfectly.

We walked to the study, waited a couple seconds for the right moment. Then I casually strolled in with my hostage in front of me.

"Hey assholes, let these people go or I'll kill your friend."

The scumbag who I thought might be the leader slowly turned. He gave me a funny look. Then he shot my hostage.

I was a bit shocked.

"Dick move," I shouted at no one specifically. It was just an observation.

He looked at me like I was a disgusting ameba under a microscope. I started feeling like maybe I did this wrong.

I took the initiative. "You know what? I bet you're not his favorite friend."

"You must be the cowboy who was in the Bentley," the man said emotionlessly.

"I'm not a cowboy... but yes. That was me. And I'm here to kick your ass. I have a hundred men on the way to back me up."

"No, you don't."

"Yes, I do." I sensed I was winning this discussion.

"You are a hired expendable and unmemorable thug this foolish woman hired to do her dirty work. And now I will kill you."

Well, shit. He's not my favorite friend either.

"Okay, look. You kill me you don't get what you're looking for. I hid it."

Jessica looked pissed off. "Shut up, Johnny. Keep your mouth shut. Don't give these commie assholes jack shit."

Commie assholes? So, *these* woman-beating butt-whistles *are* the communists who are trying to destroy America? I hate them six ways from Sunday now.

The leader turned to me with his stun gun thing. "I can make you talk as easily I am making her surrender information. I don't think you will like this. Get him, men!"

Two of his men jumped at his bark and tried to 'get' me. I decided to not cooperate. Cooperation is distasteful to me even under the best conditions. I shot them both in the face and shot their leader in the crotch.

He was dismayed.

"Kill him!" he screamed at the top of his lungs.

Suddenly it was a Chinese fire drill. I guess where they come from they just call it a fire drill, but you get the idea. I could hear the pitter patter of tiny feet and stubby peckers coming from everywhere in the house and I still had a couple of jerks in the room pulling weapons who were recovering from the shock of me shooting their boss.

I put a round in guy number one's gut. He folded. Then number two guy shot me in the arm.

Yes. It hurt. But I was in the blood lust mode now, so I ignored it and shot him dead center in the chest and as he spun around I shot him in the back of the head.

Tactical reload.

I pushed a heavy table over and took cover. Normally I don't think I could have toppled over that heavy-assed thing, but I was pumping adrenalin like a traveling salesman pumps farmers' daughters.

I blindly fired a couple of pot shots at the door to keep the invaders from bum rushing us. Then I flipped open my knife and cut Jessica's bound hands free.

As she shook free from the binding she shouted in my face. "What the hell is wrong with you? Are you mental?"

I get that a lot.

"No, I'm rescuing you."

"I didn't need rescued."

"So, should I just go home then, or shoot these guys?"

Jessica crab scooted across the floor and stole a gun off of a dead guy. She checked the weapon then fired a couple random shots at the door.

"We need to get my brother out of the line of fire then I need to question the boss. At least you didn't kill him already."

"Yeah, but he needs killing. Finish what you got to do, and I'll pop that piece of shit in the head."

I don't think Jessica was used to seeing my game face. I couldn't tell if she was more concerned with the horde of homicidal maniacs trying to murder us or with little old excessively violent me. I get a little intense after about the third guy I whack. It's like eating those cheesy snack treats. You can't stop at just one. Is it an addiction? Probably. But I don't want an intervention. It's part of my personality and I like it that way. Other than the career ending prison hitch for murdering that pervert, my intensity has served me well.

Jessica grabbed 'Mr. Leader who got shot in the nuts' guy and started slapping him like she was paint brushing a barn. I like the way she interrogates. From what I could pick up, he was spilling his guts.

While she investigated, I terminated.

Four of these little pricks tried to do a stack on our door. I think they forgot that sheet rock isn't cover, it's concealment. I could hear what they were doing and could see their shadows. They apparently weren't professionals.

I unslung my MP5 and sprayed the wall they were behind.

Screams of agony and death pierced the air.

I swear, I couldn't stop laughing.

Hal was stirring. I saw him wiggle a little and open his eyes.

I gave him a loud whisper warning, "Hal, stay down... crawl to cover."

He took my advice and wormed his way behind a heavy chair, picking up a handgun from the body of one of his tormentors on the way.

Now we had three guns if Jessica would quit farting around with Mao Tse Tung over there. When she was done we could reverse the scenario and attack. A series of cover, advance, and attack moves leapfrogging out the front door would give us room to operate. Time was of the essence. Before long it would be time for me to go do that job with Fred.

Jessica shouted, "I got it." Her words made Hal smile. I

didn't know what she got. I hoped it wasn't crabs.

"Are you done with that slob?" I asked.

"Yeah... all yours cowboy."

I executed a perfect quick-draw with my 1911 Kimber, popped him in the mouth, flipped on the thumb safety, twirled it a couple of times and jammed it back in my belt. Maybe I am a cowboy. Dino, the alpha prime Italian male of modern history, did a lot of westerns... I guess an Italian can win the west. I wondered how I'd look in a cowboy hat and boots. Probably very good. I think my classic good looks fit in any genre. I wondered if Jessica thought my classic good looks would fit in any genre. Maybe she had a thing for cowboys... I'm pretty sure I'm a cowboy now.

She duck-walked up to my position and yelled above the sporadic gunfire. "We got to get out of here."

I made eye contact with her and her brother. "On me!"

At the first lull of incoming gunfire, I gave a hand signal. We advanced in a stack with Hal and Jessica behind me laying down heavy cover fire. We got to the door and went right. I wanted to retrieve the device from its hiding place in the kitchen on the way out.

I suspected that our opponents were disoriented with their commander dead. That's the thing about these hive-think bastards with a totalitarian leader. Nobody knows how to make a decision.

They were doing more yelling at each other than shooting. That's when Hal stopped and did some dumb shit he probably saw in a movie.

"I'm not leaving with these assholes in control of my house. My kid is in there. I'm going back."

"You're gonna die too, dipshit," I very courteously advised him. "I thought you said she was safe."

"Yeah, she's tucked in like the presidential nuke shelter, but it's the idea of it"

Jessica chimed in. "He's a bit impulsive, Johnny. We better back him up."

Hal turned and dove behind a fat stuffed leather sofa. He laid flat and fired underneath it, shooting some bad guys in the feet. I had to admit. That was pretty clever. The bad guys weren't thrilled about it though.

Then he did a shoulder roll like in the movies and advanced over to an alcove where he stood and shot the wounded. Nice.

I followed. I saw some guys moving down the staircase, so I hosed them with the MP5. They left a smear of blood down the stairs as they tumbled down. I carefully aimed and fired at each of them when they stopped rolling, putting rounds in their brain pans.

One of the guy's head exploded.

Cool.

We moved through the house killing people like it was a weekend in Chicago. Without leadership, the remaining enemy agents were easy pickings. In fifteen minutes, we were done, and the property was secure.

"What about the kid?" I asked, just to be polite. I really didn't care.

Hal answered my question, "They don't have control of my house now... the fight is going on the road. She's safer if we get out of here. So, change of plans."

I made a suggestion. "How about I get the flash drive I

hid and we can still take it to the radio station."

"Maybe we go with plan B," Jessica suggested.

"I wasn't fully briefed on plan A... now you want to change?" I hate change. I was miffed.

Hal piped in the conversation, "We need to get this public."

I noticed a globe thing that was really a bar. It hadn't been shot to pieces, thankfully. I made myself a whiskey neat. This 'plan' stuff wasn't really my style. As a free thinking guy, I prefer to just do stuff and see what happens. In my experience too much thinking always backfires.

Jessica argued with her brother. "Yes, but I found out something. Something important."

"What?"

I finished my drink while I listening to the grown-up sibling rivalry shit show and made another one. I think this was some top shelf booze. But they had it in a fancy bottle so, I didn't know what brand it was. It tasted like an old single malt scotch or something... maybe it was Old Grandad... I really don't know. Then I heard her say something that caught my attention.

"He's here in LA, Hal. We can take him."

"I thought he was in New York?"

"He's here. He just flew in to take a delivery of half-billion dollar bribe money from these guys to give to American politicians. The Chinese courier will have a list outlining who in Washington and Tinseltown is on their payroll. These assholes totally stepped on their dicks this time. Some bureaucrat in Beijing wanted an accounting to make sure they weren't getting ripped off and put it all in a file. He'll have complete and irrefutable evidence of treason in his possession incriminating at least four hundred politicians and three or four hundred people here in the LA area."

"Holy shit!" Hal replied, clearly shocked at the scope and scale of the information.

"We won't even need him or the disk we have to take it all down."

Hal became enthusiastic, "Instead of his file, we'll have one straight from the Chinese leadership? The implications are almost incomprehensible."

I involved myself in the discussion, although I think they had me on ignore. "So, in what form is this half-billion dollars you speak of?"

"It's mostly US currency they've accumulated through their intellectual property and technology theft rackets. Some of it is on digital drives that access bank accounts. Why?"

"No reason." I shrugged and broke eye contact.

Jessica gave me the 'knock it off, idiot' look.

Hal spoke next, "So, where is he?"

Jessica replied, "His Beverly Hills home."

"The one we broke... I mean visited?" I asked.

"Yeah, he just got back an hour ago. Wang said so."

Wang... I snickered then came to my senses. "He's going to figure out that isn't his lock on his filing cabinet, and they'll be on high alert."

"That's okay, you'll come up with something."

"Me? I thought we were done." This was not good. "I got another job to go to tonight."

"You can be the man behind a slew of Washington politicians getting canvas bags on their heads and shipped to Gitmo."

I lit a cigarette and took a long drag. A few seconds later I blew a smoke ring toward the ceiling. "We could be there in half an hour," I estimated. "I got a plan."

We hit the armory for a re-outfitting and then fast walked toward the garage. Jessica made a phone call as we walked. Something about the garage or a garage and Beverly Hills. I supposed she was briefing her boss. If she was really a special forces soldier and her brother was really an actor, but I wasn't fully sold on any of this shit. I was just here for the money and because Jessica was hot.

A short elevator ride on the North-West-South elevator eleven or whatever got us in the cavernous car lot. We hopped into a black Cadillac. It was really more my style. The Bentley was nice but so is a Caddy for about a fourth of the money... or somewhere around a fourth to a half... Full disclosure, I don't know what either of them cost.

Hal drove this time. Jessica loaded magazines and checked weapons. I smoked a bunch of cigarettes and helped her.

Los Angeles can be beautiful at night if you don't look to closely. Much like an aging whore, she can still seduce you... although a week later your wiener might fall off. And also like an old harlot, her secrets have secrets. They say Washington is Hollywood for ugly people, and I think that might be true. But tonight, the old gal will give up her biggest secret. Who *are* the scum sucking maggots who sold out our country? I considered suggesting that they just give the list to me. For a stipend, I could probably do a better job than the cops on bringing justice to these traitors. Falls down elevator shafts and pedestrian related traffic fatalities might go up a hundred percent, but our commie problem would be solved. Still, it was probably better to focus the bright light of the law on this problem... at some point after we finish breaking a shit load of laws getting the information, of course.

The lights on the hills were mesmerizing even after all these years. I hate LA... and I love LA. I don't think it's a city, I think it's an addiction. Everyone sees themselves as the hero of their own LA story. The problem is about eighty percent of us are assholes who stayed here too long and believed that the rest of the world envied us for living here.

Hal wheeled into Beverly Hills in record time. If LA was an addictive substance, then Beverly Hills was the ultimate drug of choice. Wealth, prestige, and influence permeated the place. Even at night, it was intimidating. We negotiated the neighborhoods until we got to our target, the Coaster's, house. It was time to do some serious work now. Play time was over. The buck stops here. We're playing for keeps now... shit... I ran out of cliches... But you get the point. There are asses to kick and people to kill. And we are just the loyal citizens to do it. A movie star I never heard of, his sister the accountant Delta Force commando operating illegally spy, and me, a disgraced cop, convict, bagman. We were exactly like the three wise men of the Bible, except one was a girl and none of this had anything to do with the bible stories. Except it was close to Christmas.

We were the best America had to offer in elite deranged vigilantes. Suddenly I was very proud.

The joint was lit up like a prison during a jailbreak. I think it safe to assume he found my lock on his cabinet and figured out that the shit was about to hit the fan. The job got more complicated than I was happy with. Armed jerks were patrolling outside the estate walls and so it's reasonable to believe that armed jerks might also be *inside* the estate walls. This could amount to over a hundred armed jerks or more... according to my calculations, that was a lot of armed jerks for three vigilantes to take on.

If we were smart we'd hit it with a bazooka... jokingly, I suggested that.

"Maybe we hit the front gate with a bazooka while one of us goes in the back and takes this bastard down."

Jessica was full of surprised tonight, "Excellent idea. There's one in the trunk... but it's a Mk 153 Shoulder-Launched Multipurpose Assault Weapon, technically not a bazooka."

I can't believe these people listen to what I say. I'm almost ashamed for them.

Hal piped in, "We'll hit the front, you go in the back and get Coaster. Then we meet in his office and retrieve the evidence."

Somehow I knew this would get stupid. Rocket or not, these assholes are probably pissed off by now. We killed their sugar daddy, we stole their shit, and we are going to blow up the front of the property with a fucking missile. We'd have a serious fight on our hands.

Oh well, might as well go all in. Jessica is hot and I think she loves me, which is totally understandable.

Time to show her she made the right choice in quality handsome men to adore.

I stated my agreement, "Fine... let's see this missile thing before we roll up on these assholes."

We all got out and Hal opened the trunk with his fob. There it was... a bazooka. I don't care what she called it. I wished we had these back on the police department.

"Can I shoot it?" I asked.

"Do you know how?" Jessica countered.

"No."

"Go around back, wait for the explosion, get the guy, we'll meet you inside."

She was right.

"So, do you need him or just the list?"

"Mostly the list. The task force can take it from there without him. Although it would be ideal to question him." Jessica explained. "Don't do anything stupid or excessive, Johnny. We need a win here."

"Oh, we'll win... don't worry."

"I'm serious," she admonished.

"Fogedaboutit..." I insisted in my native language. "I got this covered. Go shoot your bazooka, little miss 'I don't let my friends shoot the bazooka,' lady."

"Are you done?" she gave me a deadpan look indicating she'd heard enough of my bullshit.

"Yeah."

"Go."

"Fine."

Our first lovers quarrel. I should make a note of the date and the time.

Hal and Jessica disappeared into the darkness with a bunch of guns and the bazooka. Alone, I wandered around to the back of the joint with my 1911, my 32, and a sweet little Daniel Defense DDM4 .300 Blackout short barrel rifle or SBR I took out of the weapons locker. The 300 Blackout round might be a little frisky for shooting in a house, but let's face it, it wasn't my house so, tough titty. I'd been wanting an SBR for a while so this would be a pleasant little test drive.

I took my time getting into position. I'd been shot once already, blown up, and my nose was still hurting, not that I'm a complainer... I just wanted to be careful, so I didn't get shot or hit so much in the immediate future. I still had to go to work tonight later. And that's three whole things that hurt.

We never really discussed at what point I was to specifically do what task when the missile went off. I was supposed to go around back and wait. But did that mean back of the outside of the house, back of the inside of the house, back of the room with the steel cabinet?

I decided it meant that no matter when the missile detonated, I'd go get some payback on the guy behind my shitty day. He was responsible for two-thirds of my current pain.

I got through the yard defense and re-shimmed the back door lock. I don't think they expected us so soon. I was able to avoid contact all the way up to the third floor with the steel cabinet.

I knew she had sent the Los Angeles County Sheriff's Office on a wild goose chase earlier. Did she have something planned for Beverly Hills PD? This was too urban.

I don't think Jessica could distract them from a bazooka fight. Still, who knows what kind of resources she or her mysterious employers had.

It was at that time that the so-called 'greatest talent agency in the world' experienced a major car fire in their underground parking garage on Wilshire.

How does she do it?

Beverly Hills has a very short list of major employers. The little city in LA, which was about ninety-percent white and ten percent Asian, was diverse in thought but not in population. After all, it was Beverly Hills. But the top employer list, which included the school district at the top followed by a handful of resorts, and then the talent agency, reflected a town of people detached from society. A protected enclave of the significantly segregated wealthy who had no residents with any practical skills. They were mostly good at play acting and screwing each other over on business deals. Patriotism and loyalty to their fellow Americans was in short supply, after all, they were far better than the rubes of the flyover states. This was Beverly Hills where even city hall cut deals with foreign countries on matters of fresh water supply, intelligence operations, and public health. I had little use for most of these Pezzos di merda.

Suddenly, the bazooka zooked… or whatever it is that bazookas do.

It was like we got nuked. The whole house shook as a blinding light flashed, then darkness, then a concussive blast that knocked me on my ass. I'm no expert but I think that was a pretty good fucking missile.

Security assholes were scrambling everywhere in the post-blast home of the Coaster, AKA, Biggest asshole in

America. I considered them targets of opportunity. What can they do to me? Shoot me with a missile and give me a sore nose? Been there and done that.

A couple of guys came up behind me with handguns at the ready.

"Hold it, asshole," one of them shouted

"Hold it yourself, I'm not gay."

I dropped like a rock, spun and fired the SBR one-handed into them full auto. Both went down. I skittered across the marble floor to a small alcove where I did a tactical magazine swap. Time to move on to the office.

Rounds started zinging around me. That hot buzzing and pop sound of supersonic lead projectiles was surrounding me like a pack of pissed off murder hornets.

I got flat on the cold marble and snaked my way to a big couch which I crawled behind and hid while assessing who in the hell was shooting at me.

It didn't matter. Jessica and Hal made entry and smoked them. I had room to operate now while they shot it out with the rest of the surviving maggots on the ground floor.

As I crawled to my target location I wondered if this blood would stain the marble floors. How would they clean it? More importantly, would they try to make me pay for it?

I got to the first door on my right in the hall. I was going to clear the room. But I didn't have to. Some asshole jumped out and tried to brain me with a big old hairy battle axe. Who has shit like that? He probably ruined the blade when he swung and missed, gouging the nice Italian marble flooring.

I had been on my side ready to push the door open when this turd appeared. Instinctively I pressed the trigger and mag-dumped his legs. I never saw him before, so let's call him shorty from here on out. I think I decapitated his right leg, if that is the right medical terminology. I'm not a doctor. I'm not required to know that shit. That's why we pay nerds to go to medical school while the rest of us go out in the world and get sick and injured.

Anyway, Shorty wasn't a happy camper. I put him out of his misery with a well-placed 45 slug to the eye and moved on. Doing another tactical reload with the rifle as I moved, I drew closer to my target.

I heard an increase in gunfire downstairs. Maybe reinforcements arrived.

It seemed safe to look, I cleared most of the floor I was on. The balcony to my left provided a good overlook to the main floor. I did a quick peek... Reinforcements did arrive... for the bad guys... well, shit!

Jessica and Hal were in the fight of their lives down there, surrounded like a potato chip dropped in the middle of a flock of seagulls.

Moving, I got into a sniper position and started tagging their most imminent threats. I shot a guy in the head who was closing on their blind side. The guy behind him took one in the throat. I have to admit, this little SBR is pretty accurate for such a short sight radius.

Something stirred behind me. A dumb ass scooting along the wall. The sound gave away his position. Even though the lighting wasn't great I could sense exactly where he was. I pulled my 1911 and emptied it into the scraping sound moving on my six. A big goon of a man collapsed behind me like a damp bag of turds on the floor, most of his face gone. Sneaky prick. He should have found a job he was better at.

I reloaded the 45.

With the threat eliminated I returned my attention to the fight below. A squad was stacking in the hall beyond their range of vision. I waited this time. As soon as all of them were visible I smoked their sorry assess with three round bursts.

I reloaded the rifle.

Between the three of us we whittled them down enough for Hal and Jessica to manage. I moved on to my primary assignment.

When I was on SWAT, many years ago, we used M4s, MP5s, and Remington 700 rifles. The M4 tended to over-penetrate interior walls so entry teams generally carried the pistol caliber carbines like the venerable MP5. What was nice about this little fight was that I didn't have to worry about over-penetration. This house had an infestation of bad guys and there were no wrong answers in firing solutions. Like Hal said earlier, just shoot until the grounds level. I was very happy right now.

I didn't get far. Four guys came down a hidden stairwell on my left. It wasn't technically hidden. It was just built in a way that a person coming down the hall wouldn't see it until they were on it. I think in architectural school they call that a design surprise or something. For me it was a shit sandwich. They were on top of me before I knew it. And they were good, at least better than most of these assholes.

The fight was so close I only had time to fire one shot

before I got punched in the head. The round hit one of them in the thigh and he fell down. It must have hurt. But why fight instead of shoot? Did they want me alive? Why?

The head punch hurt but didn't do anything. The head isn't the target you want to hit on this particular Italian if you want to take him out. I have the skull of a Caesar, a thick impenetrable head that cannot be cracked with conventional blows. Did you see Rocky? Of course, you did. I'm exactly like that.

I deflected the follow-up punch and delivered a gut sucking body shot to the closest guy. He folded and I gave him a knee to the face as I threw a brutal hook into the side of guy three's head. I felt bone crack in his melon. I think I killed him with it. I bet he was wishing he had a Caesar skull like me right now.

Guy four caught me with a punch to the ribs. It hurt but not that much. I'd worry about that one later. I countered with a rapid series of jabs before I pulled out my trusty Model 294 Buck knife and jammed the stubby blade in his clavicle.

I left it there and focused on what work was left while he yipped and did a tap dance of pain.

I yanked the trusty little 32 out of the back of my belt and popped everyone in the head who was still hopping, flopping, and dropping. I was too tired to beat them to death. This seemed like a reasonable approach to securing them. I reloaded, then stuffed my mouse gun into my hip pocket.

Being surrounded by stacks of dead enemies fortifies the soul. I got my knife back out of that one guy's shoulder, put it back in my belt, and advanced.

The target was three doors down. Almost there.

Did I mention that 'almost' only counts in horseshoes and hand grenades?

That was when I felt a shoulder hit the small of my back like a freight train hitting a goat.

Ouch!

Where in the hell did this knob come from?

It was obviously not a convenient time to get killed, so I sucked it up as I hit the deck face first, smacking my sore nose on the marble flooring. Marble is not my favorite flooring.

I was face down with a moose on my back trying to choke me out. This was not ideal. He had my arms pinned under his fat thighs as he increased pressure on my neck. Now I have a thick neck, but it isn't thick enough to prevent this guy from strangling me. My arms were behind me and I was getting murdered. Instead of fighting I relaxed. He took the opportunity to adjust his position to finish me off. I used the opportunity to get my 32 back out of my hip pocket, twist my wrist around, and launch a lead pill traveling at about 900 feet per second up his asshole.

He had a funny look on his face. His big butt acted as a suppressor, so the discharging round wasn't very loud. He didn't know exactly what happened, except it wasn't good.

Next I did a roll, counter roll and threw off his balance which allowed me to get on my back and throw a leg over his head and neck.

He might not know what happened, but I knew he was experiencing massive internal bleeding and if he lived, which he wouldn't, he would fear hemorrhoids more than he would the devil.

I was in charge now. I flipped him on his back and started delivering punches. I delivered about twenty full power hits to his face, which was now a combination of confused and mutilated. I dropped all my weight behind my forearm and smashed his windpipe. I was really doing him a favor if you think about it. His life was not going to be great after getting shot up his butt.

The excitement never ends. Two more guys were running down the hall in my direction. They were not taking prisoners. They were shooting. I got behind the maggot I just killed for cover. He absorbed their rounds quite well.

The 300 Blackout was just at the edge of my reach. I snatched it up and returned fire, smoking both of the latest threats with three round bursts.

Good times.

I could hear sustained gunfire from the last place I saw my two partners, so I knew they were still alive. Maybe they were just buying me time to complete the mission. Who knows with those types?

It was time to see Mr. Coaster or whatever the hell his name was. I moved down the hall again, this time more deliberately. I didn't want another surprise attack. My hair was a mess, my clothes were all wrinkled and bloody, and my nose hurt again. I needed to find a mirror to clean up with before I tried my most seductive moves on that hot lady soldier in my life now.

I'd get the bad guy first though.

Or should I clean up first?

I'd get him first.

I turned the corner. It was the next doorway. I could see it. And there were two final dirtbags stinking up the area in front of the target's office. Big dirtbags. Big dirtbags with rifles. These weren't the Chinese operatives. These had to be his guys. They looked like a couple of fat ugly goombahs from Brooklyn. I knew the type. Meaty foreheads, no wrists, fat un-squeezable necks, merciless, almost bulletproof, dumb as a box of dirt clods. We had guys like that on the police department. We called them motor officers.

No wonder these two didn't join the fray previously. They didn't care about the fray. They didn't care about Chinese politics. They were paid to protect my target from people like me. I had a hunch they were good at it.

Next move, negotiations.

"Hey, do you two assholes want to fight?" I yelled from behind cover. I was kind of wishing I had a 45-70 lever action right now instead of this puny 300 Blackout. It might only piss them off.

I already knew the answer to my question. Of course, they wanted to fight. But they were professionals and without saying a word, simply took positions of cover by the door.

Calling them out wasn't a good idea. I really screwed the pooch on this move. Total fail. What the hell was I thinking?

I needed a better idea.

The one thing I had going for me was that they were so big, they exceeded the size of most cover. I did a discreet pie slice peek and saw one of them had his size 17 wingtip sticking out.

Using the 45, I shot off his great toe. If you aren't familiar with technical toe names, that's the big one. He noticed.

He stood up so I blasted him with four more rounds of 45 before switching back to the rifle.

I don't think the pistol rounds affected him that much. He fell back against the wall, but was still returning fire even though seriously wounded.

I scooted back, increasing my angle of advantage and ripped a ten round burst of rifle rounds into his center mass.

I heard him grunt then I felt the house rattle as he fell flat on his back. What was that big Japanese monster called that always stomped on cities? The ground shook when it walked? It was like that. The problem was, his pal was still well concealed and prepared to kill my ass at the earliest opportunity. I was hoping he would check on his wounded friend but apparently he didn't give a shit about the other guy getting smoked. He stayed focused. I hate those kinds of people. I have trouble focusing. Focusing is like communism. Or something. It's just annoying and let's leave it at that.

One more random squirter came charging down the hall behind me. I barely looked. I just shot him in the chest. I had real problems to deal with.

Mister fortified goombah wasn't giving an inch. I couldn't get an angle on him for a shot and he had a clear fifteen foot field of fire on me.

Shit...

I totally lost sight of him. He moved. He's good.

Did he reverse? Did he know about a secret hallway

that he could access and get around behind me? That's crazy talk.

This was starting to suck.

I did another quick peek. That's when I figured out why I was about to die. The damned elevator. It's totally silent. No ding. He hopped on board, went to the second floor and came up behind me.

I knew this because I felt a massive paw grab me by the back of the head and lift me off the floor. Then I felt a series of rabbit punches in my ribs with his free hand.

He was not my favorite goombah.

I reached up and did a finger twist move to make him lose his grip on me. I only succeeded in pissing him off. He didn't let go and kept punching, which was rude.

I tried kicking out.

No luck.

I tried twisting around.

No joy.

Finally, his punching arm got tired.

He threw me down the hallway like a wet bar rag.

Breathing hurt now. I think he dinged up my ribs real good. He was quick too. He was on me in an instant.

I reached for the 45.

He slapped it away.

I reached for the 32.

He slapped it away.

I reached for my knife.

You guessed it, he slapped it away and started laughing

at me.

That sort of pissed me off. He didn't notice that I have large hands for my size. I reached between his legs and gave him the Italian nut crush. I grabbed his balls and squeezed, twisted, and ripped. I crushed his two little buddies and squeezed even harder.

His eyes widened. I had his attention. Getting my other arm free, I throat punched him as hard as I could. He fell over on his side, but I didn't let go of his crotch. I reached over and retrieved my knife and went sushi chef on his ass. I stabbed him about a hundred times and then stabbed him in the nuts.

He didn't croak yet for some reason. Oh shit, I might have really pissed him off this time.

He started to get up.

What kind of asshole gets stabbed a hundred times and gets up?

I scrambled across the marble floor on my belly and snatched up my 45. Luckily I had the foresight to top off the magazine before he turned up to put the hurt on me.

I felt the seemingly unkillable goon grab my ankle and start to pull me towards him. This guy was a monster. He was about to lean over and strangle my ass.

I didn't resist, I just let him get me close enough that I could roll around and shove my gun barrel in his mouth and mag-dump. That did the trick. He became quite peaceful. Some people aren't as unkillable as they think they are.

I collapsed on my back. Fighting makes me tired. But I wasn't done yet. The Coaster still had a reckoning due and there wasn't anything between me and his door now.

CHAPTER 11

PAIN ITALIAN STYLE

There is an Italian proverb that says, wait for the right time and place to take your revenge, for it is never well done in a hurry.

Now was the time, here was the place. Inside the room was a man responsible for corrupting my government, roughing up Jessica, and directly or indirectly causing me to get blown up earlier in the day. It was time to get some payback.

There is something these arrogant jack-offs like Coaster forget. Just because people like me are on the side of the good guys, doesn't make us good guys. Just because people like me are capable of cold blooded murder doesn't mean we don't love our country.

I'm a bad person.

I own that. I'm in my happy place there.

Now it's time to explain this little fact of life to the Coaster, the American traitor behind all the shit going down for the last twenty-five years. A bad man was going to murder him within the next five minutes.

I didn't know what to expect behind the door, but it was certainly not going to be pretty. He knew I was coming. He didn't want to lose. I'm certain he thought there was still a way out for him.

Desperate people do desperate shit. I was counting on that.

I dragged the biggest dead guy, that last monster I killed, over by the door and pushed him on his side against the wall.

My little fortification looked good enough for what I intended, but why take chances? I dragged a couple more dead maggots over and stacked them on top of his body, then I even moved a couple more behind them as a backup.

Weapons check anyone? Some of the bodies in the immediate vicinity had full mags that would work in the 1911. I had three full mags left for the SBR. I charged my weapons, straightened out my clothes, did a quick hair check in the reflection of the glass in a photo mounted on the wall, and did one more sign of the cross. This was it. Time to kill some assholes. Time to ask not what my country could do for me but who I could waste for my country... I think those were the famous words... I don't know. This just needed done. I was here to do it.

I walked down the wide hallway about fifteen feet. Turning, I ran as hard as I could and delivered the most powerful flying kick of my life at the door above the knob.

The door flew open and I dropped behind my pile of stacked bodies as an ungodly hail of raging weapon fire obliterated the entire hallway and blew out half the office wall.

I was safely tucked in behind a quarter ton of dead bad guys. They were as good at stopping bullets in death as they were in life. That didn't make the chaos any less deafening though.

I stuck my fingers in my ears until I heard the inevitable pause of dipshits reloading at the same time because they didn't function tactically.

I rolled around and killed the three dumbasses standing in the middle of the room fumbling with their weapons. They were obviously not police or military, probably just street muscle. The guy in the middle was tall, husky, had a scary neck tattoo and was dressed in black. He took two to the kisser. The guy on the right was a big fat slob with a shaved head and creepy braided go-tee beard. He took three to the guts. The last one of the three was a skinny ferret looking butt whisker in a sharkskin suit. He took one to the forehead and two to the chest.

But that's not all folks.

Bad guys number four and five came scrambling out from behind a sofa shooting and moving like professionals.

Four carried a Glock and Five had a shotgun.

I moved too. I quick crawled to behind a big chair just inside the doorway as I spray and prayed my way into the room with a little wild suppression fire.

I suppressed one guy to the pearly gates as I accidently

blew his right arm off at the elbow and then caught him with one in the side of the head. He felt that.

Fun.

I moved again to behind a couch.

Bad guy five blew the chair I was just hiding behind to pieces with a shotgun blast. I felt that was uncalled for. I popped up and fired a round with my 45, but he was diving for cover behind a wood desk. Missed.

I reloaded the SBR with a fresh mag.

"You killed my partner, you bastard!" he shouted.

"I didn't know you two were married." I countered cleverly.

"Not that kind of partner, you homophobic prick."

Great. A social justice warrior. They get offended over everything.

I replied, "Sorry. I didn't know you were a sensitive pussy either."

I think I'm winning this debate.

He yelled again, "You're going to die, asshole!"

Not the first time I've heard that one.

I decided to change my approach and give him a way out alive. Although I fully intended to shoot him in the back if he accepted my offer. "Get out of here. You don't have to die for this piece of shit. I'll let you go... just walk out."

He answered me with another shotgun blast. I'd take that as a definite 'no.'

I was safe enough this time, but I couldn't trust the couch to stop another one of those. It seemed like he was using number four shot. If he had slugs I'd be dead by now.

This guy wasn't fun anymore. I decided to end this shit and put a fresh mag in the SBR. I got to my feet and charged him, emptying the weapon into the desk. I fired on semi-automatic, shooting at a rate of about two rounds per second. I jumped up on top of the desk. He was cowered underneath it desperately wishing he had taken my previous offer.

"Okay, I quit."

He dropped his gun and put his hands up.

"Too late, dirtbag. You called me names, shot at me, you probably got overdue library books. I hate your guts now, and rightfully so. Why would I let you go?"

"Come on, man... I didn't do the uh... thing. I mean it wasn't personal."

He was losing it.

His eyes locked on mine, pleading for mercy, hoping for a shred of decency and forgiveness.

Clearly this asshole didn't know who he was dealing with. I squeezed the trigger and blew out his left eyeball. His head exploded.

Yuck.

I wondered if he realized the enormity of his fuck up in his final seconds of existence. You don't jerk around Johnny Dedd and expect to get mercy.

He was still twitching. I watched until it he went completely still. Sometimes you got to stop and smell the roses. I smelled something else. Post-mortem pants pooping.

To be fair, the whole structure smelled like death and

fire. In fact, there were quite a few fires cooking on the premises. Between the ongoing gunfire from Jennifer and Hal's part of the fight, the smoke from the fires, and the general destruction from gunfighting indoors, it felt like I was standing in the doorway to hell. We did a number on this joint. The Johnny Dedd Urban Renewal Program visits Beverly Hills. It was about time. These smug bastards were overdue for a comeuppance.

I guessed that my boy Coaster was hiding behind the big steel file cabinet.

No... not there.

Where in the hell was he?

I looked around the room. He has to be here, why would those torpedoes defended the place with their lives otherwise? The room was large, maybe twenty-five by fourteen. There was a desk, a couch that was recently shot to shit, a chair, also shot to shit, three other chairs, a table, and the cabinet. There was a bar in the corner, but it provided no form of concealment.

I could use a drink.

I walked over to the bar and poured a nice Don Camilo Anejo from its beautiful ceramic bottle into a crystal bar glass as I continued scanning the office . The Jalisco valley tequila never disappoints. I was surprised he had it. He seemed like the kind of knob who would drink a famous brand name instead the best tasting tequila. I respect his selection. He has good taste in tequila.

Meh... I'm killing him anyway.

I had to quit thinking about what was here and consider what wasn't here.

A closet. There wasn't one.

I stepped back and carefully eyeballed each of the walls. These interior walls appeared to be framed sheet-rock tape and texture walls with a tasteful light gray textured paint... now spattered with brains and blood. The ceiling was vaulted and there was a skylight centered in the room with a steel grate below it for security.

Somewhere it seemed like there should be...

There it was. A secret door in the back wall by the far corner. I could see the micro-lines now of the doorway.

I checked my rifle. Empty.

My handgun had three rounds left.

This is what I called cutting it close. The gunfire downstairs wasn't letting up, so I imagined I'd have to fight my way out after I smoke this pickle-puss pervert traitor. I'd have to make my shots count. When I was a rookie cop, my salty old field training officer told me of a time when police officers carried revolvers and loaded from loops.

How did they ever survive? That's almost like carrying a musket. But he did teach me to conserve ammo and count my shots.

But then again, he also tried to tell me they couldn't wear uniform shorts back then because their wieners would hang out, so he might have been full of shit.

It was time to get the Coaster.

With my gun in my left hand I carefully approached the hidden room.

The gunfire downstairs was becoming more sporadic, but it was still difficult to try to put my ear to the wall and listen for movement.

I ran my hand along the edge of the tiny crack in the wall. I found it. A small button at the baseboard.

I punched the button and a pocket door slid open revealing a stairwell.

Shit.

The hidden room was below this room on the second floor. Clever.

I started carefully descending the stairs taking a baby step, then listening. A baby step, then listening. The stairwell was narrow. It was about thirty-six inches wide. It wasn't an open staircase. It was closed and had a tiny landing and turn back about eight steps down. I couldn't tell if there was another door at the bottom until I cleared the turn that was four more steps down and ahead of me. He could have an army down there for all I knew. What I would give for a hand grenade right now.

Then I got one. I could hear some inconsiderate asshole opening a door. I saw that whoever that jerk was, he tossed a grenade up to the landing.

You know, sometimes I think people are just plain assholes.

Speaking of assholes, I leaped through mine and jumped like pre-surgery Kaitlin back up the stairs. I was in mid-air just through the doorway when the grenade detonated. I got a little shrapnel but nothing serious. My very excellent Italian reflexes saved my life.

Looking back down I could see the walls of the stairway were concrete covered with strips of heavy sheet metal that were concealed under the finished drywall. The grenade made a mess of it.

A serious question then occurred to me. How many grenades to they have down there? Then another question. Did they have an emergency escape hatch leading out of here?

Of course they did. That would be the only reason to risk exploding that exit.

I ran out of the room, down the hall to the stairs and hauled ass to the second floor. Sure enough, a crew was coming out of a second hidden door in the hall.

There were four huge security goons, three very young women, and a fat ugly bastard in a ten thousand dollar suit who just had to be Coaster.

And here I am with three bullets.

The only thing I had going for me was that they thought they blew me up again, which was getting to be a terrible habit they had developed over the course of the day.

I had three rounds, I used them. What was I going to save them for? Christmas?

I took aim and made head shots on three of the four goons. They went down spraying a thick gray and red aerosol of skull matter and blood over Coaster and the women.

One girl puked.

The last security guy emptied his gun at me. I had already taken cover.

He apparently was not great at gunfighting because he mag-dumped and had to reload as I charged him as fast as my tired legs would carry this handsome son of Italy.

Its interesting how fast you can run or how far you can

jump when people are trying to murder you.

I hit him with my best Oxnard High School All-State defensive lineman tackle. He felt it. He was big but I hit him hard and smashed his ass into the wall with everything I had. He dropped the gun.

There was no time to struggle for the weapon. I started punching him hard... repeatedly... viciously on or about the face and head until my hands hurt.

He slumped to the floor.

Shit. I beat him to death with my bare hands.

Coaster was in shock. He had never seen anything like that. He was a behind the scenes backstabbing pervert and worm. He wasn't man enough to face danger. He was perhaps the most worthless puke of a man ever born. Using the power of media to destroy his own country from within at the direction of a foreign foe was sickening for a normal person to even think about.

I saw him glance down at goon four's gun on the floor. It was about six feet away from him. Maybe twelve feet from where I stood. He glanced back at me. He was going to do something.

Then it got stupid.

CHAPTER 12

PAINDEMIC

I think he thought he could get to the gun before I could stop him. I had to agree with him on that. But did he know how to use it if he got it? It was a Glock, point fire, no safety. Essentially it was a semi-auto wheel gun with high capacity, flat and compact, and no drama.

He could totally operate it. Anyone could.

Shit.

Then the next asshole shows up.

Out of the secret exit a middle-aged woman emerged carrying a very large leather valise that looked like an old doctor's bag, a backpack, and a gun. She was Asian, perhaps fifty-years old and looking fine. I was only late thirties, but I'd ask her out in a heart-beat. She was built like a top-tier pole-dancer and had the face of an angel. A murderous angel with a Sig 365 in her hand.

"Don't try anything, asshole," she warned.

I wondered if we had met. She seemed to know the key feature of my personality. I took her advice and didn't move.

Coaster seemed desperate, yet at the same time, relieved she was there. "Do you have it all?"

"Of course, darling. What did you think? I have a million cash, drives with the access codes to the full half-billion, and all our blackmail packs to keep our little minions on track."

"Perfect." He suddenly seemed unduly pleased with himself even though he didn't seem to be adding any value to the proposition at this time. "Kill him and let's go," he ordered, pointing at me.

Did you ever notice how the absence of sound is sometimes louder than the sound of silence? The gunfire downstairs had stopped. I noticed it. I don't think my two scumbag friends here did though.

I sensed movement behind me. Somehow I knew it wasn't malevolent. The faint essence of her perfume told me that Jessica was behind me. In my peripheral vision I saw Hal.

This was no time to talk. It was time to shoot. Hal figured out what I had going on in here almost immediately, but he didn't make the right move. There is a time to talk and a time to shoot. This was the time to shoot.

"Drop your weapon," he yelled at the woman. "Get back, Johnny."

Shit, he should have just popped her, and we'd be done. Instead she snap fired a shot at him and ran down the hall in the opposite direction with the bags and evidence.

I saw Hal drop. I could see it wasn't the first time he got shot this evening. This last bullet certainly didn't help his overall well-being. He bravely, or foolishly depending on who is telling it, took a bullet while trying to get me to safety rather than just shooting that woman like the dirty dog she was. Now I owed him.

Owing people isn't my favorite thing.

I was standing there in the middle of this latest shit show when Coaster bum rushed me, throwing his bulk into my chest, and knocking me backwards. Jessica dashed around us in pursuit of the woman, leaving her wounded brother to die in the hall. I thought that was hard-core. Maybe she really was Delta Force.

The fat turd knocked the wind out of me with his unexpected tackle. I was already hurting anyway. I was physically tired too. This was not an ideal way to wrap up the evening.

He could tell I was hurt. Coaster turned away and went for the gun. I stuck my foot out and tripped him. I wasn't *that* hurt. He fell flat on his face. With what I had left, I got to my knees and threw a full power elbow into the middle of his back.

I heard him wheeze in pain as the air sucked out of his lungs and as his entire nervous system lit up like some comedian dropping an M-80 down the back of your pants. His neural system was totally overwhelmed with the stun blow I delivered. He quivered and involuntarily peed his pants. You've heard of Greco-Roman wrestling? That was a Roman move. It was all us. We invented that shit. It works.

I glanced up to see Hal trying to crawl toward us, struggling to get to his feet.

Then he collapsed. He didn't look too good.

I heard the crack of a rifle round at the end of the hall and around the corner. I hoped it was Jessica smoking that commie woman. She was hot but there some lines you don't cross and expect to live. China lady crossed them all

I staggered to my feet.

Coaster muttered something as he continued reaching for the gun on the floor. "You bastard!"

I hate being insulted. Especially by a traitor. But I thought I'd wait and see where he was going with this thought.

"You'll pay," he threatened with venom oozing thickly out of each word.

"No, I won't," I countered.

"Yes, you will."

I felt like I was winning this argument.

I staggered along, standing over him, as he slithered over to the weapon like a worm, reaching for it with his outstretched hand.

He was brushing the side of the grip with his fingertips. Close but not quite there.

With the toe of my shoe, I kicked him hard in the ribs until he rolled over on his back.

Rage turned his face into a distorted mask of hate. He decided to run his mouth some more. "Johnny, is that what she called you? You're dead, Johnny. You are dead."

He tried to sound menacing. I wasn't menaced. I was pissed.

I stood over him, wounded and tired. It was time to end it.

"Funny... You're almost right.:"

"What?" it was obvious that my answer confused him.

"Yeah... my name is Johnny. Johnny Dedd. I hurt people for money. Sometimes I kill people for money. Other times I just kill people who need killing. You are a rodent, a traitor, and a maggot. You need killing."

His eyes widened. He finally began sensing that there might be no way out of this. He had dodged consequences his entire life. Now the force of good, delivered by an evil man, would send him to the hell he belonged in.

I relished his terror.

"Coaster." I said, ready to pronounce sentence on this dirtbag.

He interrupted me. "You can let me go, Johnny. I can make you rich. I can make you famous. Women. Money. Everything. Just don't hurt me," He pleaded.

His begging was disgusting as he was. I smiled. "No Coaster... I don't think so. But I'll tell you what I *will* do."

"What? Anything."

"I'll tell you the future. That should be worth something."

"What?" Confusion now dominated his face. He was the guy who set terms... he called the shots... now he wonders, who is Johnny Dedd and why does he have to kill me?

"This is what will happen in the next five seconds."

"What the hell is wrong with you? What are you saying?" he screamed in desperation.

I stayed calm. I gave my prediction.

"I see you accused of treason. I see you labeled a coward. I see you being known worldwide as worthless piece of shit. And for all your evil intentions... there is a price to be paid."

I paused and let him see my teeth. Let him see *my* hate.

"I stomp on your throat."

There is a look a man gets on his face when he knows he's screwed. It's a combination of horror and surrender. Finality and failure. It's the end of breathing, seeing, and being.

Coaster had that look.

I stomped on his throat.

It was satisfying to feel the larynx crush under my heel, to flatten his neck into the cold marble floor, to watch this dirtbag croak. I kept my foot there until he stopped wiggling, his eyeballs rolled back, and he looked at me with that glassy-eyed half-lidded stare of the dead.

I wiped my foot off on his chest and walked over to check on Hal.

"Thanks for the warning, buddy...

"It's what friends do, Johnny."

He called me friend. I hadn't had that happen in a long time. He probably didn't mean it, but it was an unexpected emotional experience to hear it. Maybe I did want a friend. Maybe I'd buy a cat.

"How bad is it?" I asked as I checked his wounds.

"I'm fine, just shot up a little. Nothing I can't handle."

Over my shoulder I saw movement. It was Jessica

carrying her rifle, the backpack, and the bag.

She asked, "How is he?"

"He's okay. We need to get him home and fixed up though. Where's the Asian lady?"

"I blew that sorry bitch's head off. She was the local Chinese State Security Ministry's head agent for the United States. I retired her ass early."

"Nice... will that cause problems?" I asked.

"After this, you call that a problem?" she countered.

"I see your point." I deferred to her wisdom.

"What happened to Coaster?"

"He choked on a mouthful of treason."

"That shit happens." She said with a near smile.

"yeah, nobody knows why... it just happens some-times."

"Let's get Hal home," she said. "This job is a wrap."

CHAPTER 13

PAINFUL PAIN

We got Hal situated and stabilized. He had a couple of in and out wounds but was otherwise going to be fine. A private doctor showed up after Jessica made a couple of mysterious phone calls. The doc was a strange little guy, but he seemed to know what he was doing. He gave Hal an injection and he was up and talking like nothing happened just a few minutes after the doc treated his wounds.

Hal was good. I was okay. Jessica was still hot. There was nothing left to do here.

"Let's step into the den, Johnny," she suggested.

We walked back into the den and she made us a couple of cocktails. I sensed she had something to say to me. I wasn't sure I was ready to listen. I was hoping that I hadn't misread this evening's activities and that now she was going to read me my rights or something.

She spoke softly as she handed me a whiskey on the rocks... the way I like it... Whiskey and the rocks on the side. "Johnny, you've had a rough patch the past few years."

Where was this going? "What? What do you know about me? I'm fine."

"Look, I know of a Foundation, sort of a secret organization, that could use a guy like you. They handle problems... more or less in a similar manner to the way you do. You could be one of the good guys again."

I took one drink and then another before responding. "I crossed a line a long time ago, Jessica. I'm where I belong. Thanks, but no thanks. Johnny Dedd isn't looking for a job."

"If you change your mind, let me know. The offer stands." She extended her index finger in the air like she just remembered something important, "Wait here."

She disappeared for a maybe three minutes at the most. She came back with a Ziplock bag containing about two-hundred thousand bucks. "Your commission plus bonus."

"I earned it." I said with a wink as I took the money and set it on the table beside me. It made her smile. She had a beautiful smile. I posed a question. "You know, you could answer something for me, Jessica."

"My name isn't really Jessica."

"I didn't think it was. Who are you?"

"I'm the best woman you'll never know, Johnny."

She grabbed me by the hair with one hand and the

Toscano Salami with the other while laying the lip-lock of my life on my irresistible Italian lips.

She leaned back. We stared at each other for a long instant then I kissed her back, hard on the mouth.

As I put my arms around her, I noticed my watch. It was midnight. Time to help Fred Herst. Shit… "Baby I got to go to work."

"Are you serious?" she asked half angrily, yet her eyes were reflecting a hint of mirth.

I think she appreciated my bullshit. That requires a woman of quality.

I explained, "I got a reputation in this town, Jess… or whoever you are. A jobs a job."

"But your half dead."

"No, baby… I'm Johnny Dedd…" I put my left hand to my ear in the universal phone position. "Call me."

I grabbed my bag of money and headed for the door.

"See you again, Johnny." She called out as I left.

"Twenty-five thousand in advance is the fee." I replied as I disappeared into the night.

EPILOGUE

A month after I wasted Coaster, a FedEx package arrived at my house at nine AM on a Tuesday morning... I had to sign for it. I wasn't expecting anything.

Inside was a full presidential pardon, a letter restoring my rights, a new carry permit, and a very strange job offer letter. I put it away and went to an appointment with my hair stylist. The mystery paperwork could wait. It's important to look good.

I'm Johnny Dedd... Remember that shit.

ABOUT THE AUTHOR

Bronco Hammer

Bronco Hammer, a son of Texas, is a mysterious and complex individual. He currently spends his days enjoying a cold beer, while writing books aboard a boat near Coronado, California. That is about all you need to know.

Oh... You think you need to know more? Fine... His interests include trucks, boats, horses, guns, sandwiches, and science.

Order action novels by Bronco Hammer at amazon.com/author/broncohammer

Stay in Touch
Bronco Hammer can be contacted at the Bronco Hammer Briefing Room at broncohammer.com

About Dan - Senior Creative Consultant
After retiring from a twenty-three year law enforcement career, Dan focused his attention on various endeavors

that remain classified to this day, mainly because he forgot most of them.

PRAISE FOR AUTHOR

DIE YOU COMMIE BASTARDS
I knew Bronco Hammer when he was merely a "slightly per-
ilous" author. I followed his career and have seen his written
works push him into becoming "The Most Dangerous Writer
in the World."

But it's NOT all about HIM! For example, when I finished "Narc
in the Dark", I noticed my shirt sleeves tightening up around
my biceps. At the completion of "Hollywood Scum Must Pay",
I dropped two waist sizes in my jeans (AND had to remove all
the sleeves from my wardrobe!). By the time I finished "Die
You Commie Bastards" and "Pimps Must Die", I started bench
pressing small, lightly armored vehicles AND was declining
"Friend" and "Follow" requests from supermodels on a daily
basis. When I finished "Man Of Violence" I just gave up on
wearing cologne, 'cause there wasn't a need for it anymore. So
not only is he the "Most Dangerous" writer, he's also the most
generous by sharing the secrets of "He-Manning" to readers
galaxy-wide.

- ARLYN WALZ

SPANK ME WITH A DEAD MIDGET
Bronco Hammer has his finger on the pulse of the American Male and the action hero genre! He just has to be careful because his fingers are registered as deadly weapons and he could easily erase any human being's place at the Thanksgiving Day dinner table should he use that finger for evil. I found myself immersed in a story that had me identifying with the main character as only I could. Spank Me was definitely a page turner until I reached the last page. Then I had to stop because, well it was the end! Great read!

- JOHN ROLFE

MAN OF VIOLENCE
"Man of Violence" is as American as apple pie!

- JOHNNY DEE

PIMPS MUST DIE
Bronco Hammer books bring out the beast in men and the super model in women. If all Americans read his books, we wouldn't need a military. His writings are filled with action, humor and more action. Then more humor. Hammer is a genius. He paid me to put that last sentence in. I would have said it anyway, but since he paid me don't tell him I said that.

Hollywood Scum Must Die and Spank Me with A Dead Midget

are recommended first reads for beginners.

- RANDY LEWIS

HOLLYWOOD SCUM MUST PAY
The first time I read a Bronco Hammer book, I was hooked. He creates the most outlandish characters I have ever read about. I love a book that makes me laugh out loud and I had tears in my eyes during the first chapter.

Bronco's books are full of action, wit, humor, and surprises. I'll never forget a police office telling a lawyer that, "She hit me with a poodle." And the story only got funnier after that. Bronco Hammer books are for real men and women. Wimps should not to read them. They wouldn't understand.

- ELVIS BRAY

MAN OF VIOLENCE
Cancel your gym membership. Forget working out. Bronco Hammer novels will get you in shape pronto. The most exciting and testosterone inducing writer in the world.

- PAUL KENNEDY

SPANK ME WITH A DEAD MIDGET
Trigger Warning! Just kidding, if you need a trigger warning you're not man enough to read a Bronco Hammer book!

However, be prepared after reading just one book for any bottled water you have in your house to be turned into whiskey. You will probably wake up with a full beard and a sleeve tattoo upon reading the words of Bronco Hammer!

After the second Bronco Hammer novel I read, I had to call the Police to remove all the women from my front porch who were trying to get in to see me, and my reading material!

I also became a better shot and all of my guns had greater stopping power after reading these literary masterpieces! Bronco Hammer books are like a magic elixir for your manhood, read one today....if your man enough!

- S. DAYTON

Bronco Hammer books put hair on your chest and weeds out the cry babies.

- SAMI JO FIFE - SPEAKING ON BEHALF OF HER HUSBAND'S CHEST